FiSH FiNelli

BOOK 1

FOR NIKO - E.S.F.
Special thanks to Craig Virden, Fish's first fan;
CNP, who told me about seagulls and pickles;
Steve T for lit crit; Debbie, a fab cheerleader;
JRS, my dad, and everyone at the East Hampton Library—
Dennis, Lisa, Alex, Jane, Lisa K, Sheila, Gina, Chelsea;
and Steve B for maps.

FOR MY EXPLORERS: FABIOLA AND MIRABELLE - J.B.

Text © 2013 by E.S. Farber.
Illustrations © 2013 by Jason Beene.

Library of Congress Cataloging-in-Publication
Data available.
ISBN 978-1-4521-0820-9

Design by Amy Achaibou and Lauren Michelle Smith.
Typeset in Century Schoolbook.
The illustrations in this book were rendered digitally.

MIX
Paper from
responsible sources
FSC® C008047
www.fsc.org

Manufactured in China.

10 9 8 7 6 5 4 3 2 1

Chronicle Books LLC
680 Second Street, San Francisco, California 94107

www.chroniclekids.com

SEAGULLS DON'T EAT PICKLES

BY E.S. FARBER • ILLUSTRATED BY JASON BEENE

chronicle books·san francisco

CODE ORANGE

It all started the morning I broke into my lobster piggy bank. I had chosen a basin wrench for the job. It's a good tool for a delicate operation. I know this because my dad is a plumber and taught me lots of stuff about tools.

CLINK! CLINK! I shook the lobster a few times.

It sure sounded like there was a lot of money in there. I hoped it was at least $54.53. That was exactly how much I needed to buy the Seagull. In case you're wondering, the seagull I'm talking about isn't the aquatic bird. It's one of the finest motor boat engines ever made. And I had to get it soon. See, I've been fixing up this boat with my best friends, Roger and T. J. We want to race it in the Captain Kidd Classic, the biggest boat race of the summer.

I held the lobster bank with my fingers over the part on the shell that read *Lobster-Palooza—Where Lobsters Rock!*

The Lobster-Palooza festival happens every summer in our town of Whooping Hollow. I won the lobster bank for bringing in a blue lobster I caught with my Uncle Norman. Only one in about three million lobsters is blue, by the way.

I put the gripper end of the wrench into the Lobster-Palooza lobster's pincer claw. I pulled gently. Nothing happened, so I pulled a little harder.

CRACK! The pincer claw snapped off. Money flew in the air.

PLOP! Dimes and pennies landed in the fishbowl. Nikola Tesla, my goldfish, started swimming around like crazy. As I was fishing the coins out of Nikola Tesla's bowl, I heard a scream. "Help! Ugly-Buggly!"

"Fish!" my mom called up the stairs. "Help your sister, please. I'm baking!"

My real name is Norman, by the way, but I've been called Fish ever since I can remember. Uncle Norman, who I'm named after, said it was my first word. I was on his boat when an angry bluefish took a chomp out of his finger. I laughed and said "Fish."

"Aaahhh!" my four-year-old sister, Feenie, shrieked again.

I took off down the hall.

"It's in there!" said Feenie, moving her arms so her fairy wings flapped up and down like she was trying to fly. "And it's the biggest one ever!"

The Ugly-Buggly jumped out from behind the toilet. It was huge. Bigger than a praying mantis, with long brown tentacles and legs as fat as noodles. I didn't want to tell Feenie, but she was right. It was the biggest one I'd ever seen. I definitely needed help.

I raced back to my room. Dude, our old black cat, was sleeping on my bottom bunk. "I'm on a mission, Dude, so scram!" Dude gave me a look, but he hopped off the bed. I reached under the mattress and pulled out my walkie-talkie. I pressed the PTT (Push To Talk) button.

"Roger," the walkie-talkie crackled to life.

I peered out my bedroom window, which looked right into Roger's

WALKIE-TALKIE

Developed during World War II for military communications via air waves, it was both a transmitter and a receiver that weighed about 35 pounds and was carried like a back-pack. Today it has a half-duplex channel so only one radio can transmit at a time, although many can listen.

bedroom window. We've been next door neighbors for almost ten years, ever since we were born.

"This is Roger!" came Roger's staticky, walkie-talkie voice. "Do you read me?"

"Read and copy!" I said.

"Whale Creek in fifteen?"

"Sure, but Roger—"

"Roger, ten-four, over and out," said Roger's staticky voice.

"Roger, no," I said. "Roger, it's—"

"Roger that!" said Roger. "Over and—"

"No, Roger, I mean *you*, Roger, not roger," I said.

"Oh," said Roger. "Roger."

"Will you stop rogering me, Roger?" I said.

"Wilco," said Roger.

"We've got a situation!"

"What level?" asked Roger.

"Code Orange!"

"I'm there," said Roger. "Secure the prisoner. You know, I got your back, dude."

"Speaking of backs, don't forget the Bug Patrol Emergency Backpack!"

"Roger, over and out!" said Roger.

UGLY-BUGGLY

When I got back to the bathroom, Feenie was waving her magic wand up and down in front of the shower curtain.

"What are you doing with that wand?" I asked. "Trying to make the bug disappear?"

"As if," said Feenie. "I'm only a FAPIT, you know."

"What's a FAPIT?" I shouldn't have asked.

"Fairy Princess in Training," said Feenie. "See, to *disaway* something you need to be a FUFAP, you know, a Full Fairy Princess."

"*Disaway* is not a word, Fee."

"Is so," said Feenie, nodding her head up and down so hard her pigtails flew up beside her ears. "It's a magic word."

"What does it mean then?"

"You have to be a FAPIT to understand," said Feenie.

"Oh, brother," I said.

The back door slammed and Roger appeared at the top of the stairs. He was lugging an orange backpack with a big sticker of a tooth on it that read KEEP YOUR SMILE IN STYLE. He got it the last time he went to the dentist and had ten cavities.

"We need a Number Three," I said.

"Number Three?" asked Roger, his brown eyes widening. "We've never had a Number Three before."

"I told you it was a Code Orange."

But when we got back to the bathroom, the tub was empty. The three of us eyed one another.

"Where'd it go?" whispered Feenie.

"Down the drain?" said Roger.

"Impossible," I said. "All insects have exoskeletons, you know, skeletons on the outsides of their bodies. So no way a big one, like an Ugly-Buggly, can squeeze through tiny holes like there are in a drain."

"Fish, how could you forget the most important rule of Bug Patrol Operations?" said Roger. "Never underestimate the sly and sinister mind of a creepy-crawlie." He pulled back the shower curtain.

The Ugly-Buggly hopped out from behind a fold. We all jumped.

"Aaahhh!"

"See, super-sly, just like I told you." Roger turned to the bug. "Okay, Ugly-Buggly, we've got you surrounded. It's white flag time."

Roger reached into the back-pack and pulled out a magnifying glass, a pair of scissors, and a half-eaten tuna sandwich. The whole bathroom suddenly stank like rotten fish.

"Pee-yew!"

WHITE FLAG

Waving something white is the worldwide symbol of surrender. It started way back in ancient China and Rome. When one side didn't want to fight anymore, they would wave something white on a stick. It was way easier for the other side to see than putting your shield over your head.

"So *that's* what happened to my lunch," said Roger. Next he pulled out a jumbo-sized Cheezy Cheezers container. It had a number three on it.

"Containment Sealer Device?" I asked.

"Right here," said Roger. He took out a piece of pink notebook paper with a heart on it that read *Beck, you rock!* "It's Summer's love letter to Beck Billings. Perfect Containment Sealer Device, right?"

"How did you get it?" I asked. I had a hunch that Summer, who was Roger's older sister, would not be happy to know we were about to use her private love letter to trap an Ugly-Buggly. Beck happens to be Bryce Billings's older brother and a star lacrosse player, and every girl at Marine Middle has a crush on him.

"I found it in her trash," said Roger. "And I figured, hey, 'Reduce, reuse, recycle.' Just trying to help save the planet."

Driving Summer crazy was one of Roger's favorite pastimes.

"I'll handle the container, you back me up with the Containment Sealer Device," said Roger.

"How about if I do the container and you—"

The bug jumped again.

"Aaahhh!"

Roger held up the Cheezy Cheezers container. Then he plopped it over the bug.

I picked up the pink paper and took a deep breath. Slowly, I slid the Containment Sealer Device toward the container where the Ugly-Buggly was hopping like crazy, trying to get out.

"On three," I said to Roger. "One . . . two . . . three!"

Roger lifted up the container as I slid the paper underneath. We watched for a moment as the bug hopped up and down on Summer's heart.

"Mission accomplished," said Roger. "It's time for the release."

I stood up carefully, my hand keeping the Containment Sealer Device in place. Roger was next to me, his hand on top of the container. Slowly we walked out of the bathroom. Side by side, we started down the stairs.

"Open the door, Feenie!"

Feenie ran ahead. Roger and I followed her across the hall. The door was open. We were almost there when there was a bark. Something large, pink, and fluffy bounded into the room.

"What happened to my dog?" I said, staring at the pink princess quilt tied around him with a jump rope.

"Woof!" barked Shrimp, wagging his long brown and white tail. Everything about Shrimp is big. We didn't know he was part Saint Bernard when we got him as a puppy.

"He's not a dog," said Feenie. "He's a magic horse."

Just then Shrimp started sniffing like crazy. He looked at our outstretched hands. He saw we were holding something. He sniffed the air. He stared at Roger. *Oh, no,* I

thought. The tuna fish sandwich! It was in the backpack on Roger's back.

"Don't, Shrimp!" I said.

But it was too late. Shrimp jumped and knocked into Roger. The container flew out of his hand.

THE TREASURE IS PLASTIC?!

It took us three tries to get that Ugly-Buggly out of the house. It was a record, even for a Code Orange. After that I headed back up to my room to count the money that had fallen out of the lobster bank. I piled it up in stacks— quarters, dimes, nickels, pennies. And three dollar bills. I counted it slowly and carefully.

$27.51! *What???!!!*

I counted it again. $27.51. The Seagull motor cost $54.53. That meant I needed a whole $27.02. *Whoa!*

I sighed and slid down the banister. I had to think of some way to get $27.02 fast, or the summer would be over. But how???

"Mom, I'm going to Whale Creek," I said as I walked into the kitchen.

Whale Creek isn't really a creek, by the way. And the water is much too shallow for a whale to swim in it. But it's right by the cove that leads to Whooping Hollow Harbor, where there's a giant boulder that people used to stand on to look for whales. If somebody spotted one, they would climb a tree and wave their shirt around and yell, "Whale off!" Then the settlers in the town and the Native Americans would go harpoon it. They would split up the whale meat and the blubber (*good for oil to light lamps*) and this weird stuff ambergris (*used to make perfume*) and the teeth and bones (*good for carving*).

"Take Feenie with you," said my mom, just as Roger skateboarded through the back door.

"Aw, Mom."

"Fish, my soufflé needs quiet," said my mom, with a protective glance at the oven. "Or it will fall."

"No problem, Mrs. F.," said Roger. "Heave-ho, ready to go?" He waved his pirate sword and grinned at Feenie.

"*Mom*," I said. "She'll just get in the way."

"Fish!" said my mom, giving me her stingray glare. When she does that, I know she means business.

"All right, but you have to be the prisoner on the pirate ship," I told Feenie.

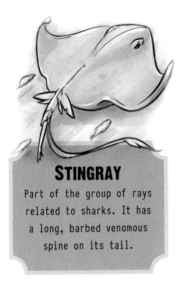

STINGRAY
Part of the group of rays related to sharks. It has a long, barbed venomous spine on its tail.

"FAPITs can't be prisoners," said Feenie.

"Don't worry, Mrs. F.," said Roger. "I won't let any evil pirates hurt a hair on her lovely head."

My mom smiled. So did Feenie. I rolled my eyes as I grabbed my skateboard and my sword. I'd made it myself out of plywood, with duct tape for the hilt.

As soon as we got outside, Roger pushed off and ollied down the curb. I jumped on my board and pushed off after him. Shrimp barked and lunged after me.

"Wait for me!" called Feenie.

I looked back. She was still standing in front of our house with one foot on her scooter.

"I'd better pull you," I said. "Or the tide will get there before we do."

I took the rope out of my pocket and tied it around my waist. Then I tied the other end to the scooter.

"Hold on tight!" I said.

Off we went to the end of Cinnamon Street. Shrimp barked and raced around us.

"Dude, I beat your best time by five whole seconds," said Roger when we got up the hill at the end of Red Fox Lane. He pointed to his stopwatch.

"I'm not racing, Roger," I said, trying to catch my breath. "I'm towing."

"Safety first!" said Feenie, flapping her fairy wings.

"Safety first!" came a high, squeaky voice from somewhere close by.

"Who said that?" asked Feenie.

"Me!" Mmm popped up from behind the Mahoneys' fence. She was wearing sparkly wings just like Feenie's. "I'm a FAPIT!"

"I'm a FAPIT, too!" said Feenie.

Mmm's real name is Margaret Mary Mahoney, but she's been called Mmm since she was born. Margaret was too hard for her brothers T. J. and Mickey to say.

"Where's T. J.?" I asked.

"Doing something to his bike," said Mmm.

T. J. was always doing something to his bike. He has this old ten-speed his dad picked up on a carting job. I helped him put new spokes on the wheels. But he's always getting flats, and then we have to patch the tires.

As if he had supersonic hearing and could hear us talking about him, T. J. came wheeling his bike down the driveway.

"I was about to look for you guys," said T. J. He took a bite out of a mushy candy bar that looked like it had taken a trip through the washing machine. "Check it out," he said, nodding his curly red head at a gray box strapped to the back of his bike.

"What's in it?" I asked.

"Treasure," answered T. J., wiping chocolate off his mouth with his sleeve.

"Come on, T. J.," I said. "The only treasure that's buried anywhere near here is Captain Kidd's, and nobody's ever found it."

Some people say it's buried on Lyons Island, where Captain Kidd landed, right across the harbor from Whooping Hollow. Some say it's near the old lighthouse at the bottom of Money Pond, which is bottomless and why the treature's never been dug up. Lots of treasure hunters have hunted for it for years and years. It's the biggest unsolved mystery in Whooping Hollow.

"Well, it looks like I just did," said T. J. "I was at the

mall with my dad. He was hauling up the dumpster, and there it was."

"You're telling me you found Captain Kidd's treasure at the mall?!" said Roger.

"Uh-huh."

I eyed the box. "But it's plastic. A real treasure chest isn't made of plastic."

"Oh, yeah?" asked T. J. "If what's inside this box isn't treasure . . . I'll eat my . . . hat."

He popped open the lock on the chest. Our eyes opened wide. The chest was filled with gold.

"Snap!" said Roger. "We're rich!"

"Hold your horses, guys," I said, picking up a gold coin. It was plastic, just like the chest. In tiny letters on the bottom it read MADE IN CHINA.

"It's from China, T. J.," I said.

"China?" said T. J. "China's those plates and teacups and stuff that me and Mickey and Mmm aren't supposed to touch."

Roger and I laughed. "It's not china like dishes," I said. "These gold coins are made in China, the country China, as in on the continent of Asia near Japan. Home of Confucius and Jackie Chan and the Great Wall, the place where gun

powder was invented, and the abacus and wonton soup. Get it?"

"Oh," said T. J., chewing on some licorice. "Wonton soup's okay, but I like egg rolls better."

"The point is that these coins were made in China," I said.

"They're still gold, though, right?" He winked at me.

"Not real gold," I said. "Plastic molded and painted to look like gold."

T. J. ate the rest of his licorice while he digested this information. "But just because they're plastic doesn't mean they're not treasure, right? 'Cause I sure don't want to eat this stinky old baseball cap."

ARE YOU *CAPTAIN KIDDING ME?*

The boat was anchored at the foot of the Captain's dock. It's an old whaler that needs some work and a new motor, which is why I'm saving up for the Seagull, but it's light and fast and can hold a lot of weight. The Captain says a whaler can still float after taking a thousand rounds of weapons fire, and can even run if it's cut in half. (Of course, you have to have the half with the motor.) He says I can have it, once I get my Boating Safety Certificate next month when I turn ten and learn how to navigate with a compass. Then he's going to give me the same test his dad gave him, like, a hundred years ago, before whaler boats were even invented.

Everyone stopped by the dock. It goes all the way out to Whale Rock, right by the cove, so you can see all the boats going by. It's just about my favorite spot in the world. I walked around the back of the house and looked up. The Captain wasn't on the widow's walk at the very top. Only his telescope was. His house is really old. It belonged to his grandpa's grandpa, who was a whaler and used to go on voyages to hunt for whales. His grandma's grandma used to walk on that very widow's walk, looking for his ship.

"Let's get this party started, Fish!" called Roger.

I ran up the porch steps and picked up a long wooden paddle that was hanging from a string off an old bronze gong. The Captain traveled a lot in his Navy days. He brought the gong all the way back from Madagascar (that's an island in the Indian Ocean near Africa, by the way). I hit the gong with the paddle and jumped back.

BONG! BONG! BONG! I covered my ears. That thing is so loud, it makes my teeth rattle.

A minute passed and then another. POP! A bright red streak shot over our heads. It was a flare, just like the flares they used at sea when the Captain was in the Navy. The Captain loves to set off flares. Sometimes I think he forgets he's living in a house and not on a ship.

The flare is our signal.

"Finally," said Roger. "Let's go, mateys."

"Not so fast, Rog," I said. "We need PFDs."

"Oh, good, snacks," said T. J. "I never heard of Peefdees. Are they a new kind of potato chip?"

Roger laughed. "They're life jackets, dude, not part of any food group."

"You mean Personal Flotation Devices," I corrected. The one time I forgot, the Captain got so mad he actually shot off his cannon.

The Captain kept the PFDs in an old wooden shed by the dock. I pulled out two small ones for the girls and three bigger ones for Rog, T. J., and me. The Captain has lots of boating equipment from when his kids were kids. He always tells me so long as I keep things shipshape, I can use whatever I want.

The girls sat in the middle of the boat, waving their wands around. They looked kind of funny with fairy wings poking out of their PFDs. At least they were wearing the life jackets.

We pulled the boat out as far as the anchor would let it go. "I am Captain Terrible Teeth," said Roger, sticking his plastic vampire teeth in his mouth. "I am here to rescue you ladies!"

"Aaahhh!" they screamed.

"You don't stand a chance against Captain Kidd, the bravest pirate hunter of the seven seas," I said. "Now get in and paddle, Terrible Teeth!"

Roger growled, but he hopped in and picked up the old oar we used as a paddle.

"My spyglass, Smee!" I nodded at T. J. "I think I see a sail to starboard."

"I bet it's a ship flying the Jolly Roger flag here to rescue me," said Roger. "Get it? Jolly Roger? Roger!"

T. J. held out the telescope we keep in a bag under the seat. The box of plastic gold was right beside it.

"Not so fast, Terrible Teeth," I said. "This gold is ours."

"Oh, yeah, Kidd?" said Roger. He hopped up and brandished his sword. "I challenge you to a duel."

"I accept," I said, whipping out my sword.

"Hey, Kidd, I see a boat on the horizon," said Roger.

"You just don't want to duel, you coward."

"I'm not kidding. A boat is coming all right."

I made my way to the bow and looked through the telescope. Sure enough, a boat was coming toward us through the harbor. It was white with a bright green stripe and it was moving fast. The waves it made rocked our boat.

"To starboard!" I told T. J., so we could get a better look.

"Starboard?" asked T. J.

"Right," I said.

"Right?"

"Right!"

"Right, what?" T. J. cocked his head, confused.

"Turn the wheel to the RIGHT!" I ordered. "That's what starboard means."

T. J. yanked hard on the wheel. The boat turned so fast, it almost flipped over.

"Aaahhh!"

Roger whistled. "Check out this baby! I bet she's got twenty horsepower!"

"What do horses have to do with it?" asked T. J., popping a jelly bean in his mouth.

"I bet they're magic horses," put in Feenie.

"Horsepower isn't magic, it's a measure of power," I said. "See, if the motor is twenty horsepower, it means it has the power of twenty horses. To really figure it out, you'd need to know the size of the horse and—"

"What the heck, Fish?!" interrupted Roger. "Who's at the wheel?" He lunged for the telescope.

The boat rocked and the girls screamed. T. J. dropped his jelly beans into the water.

"Don't, Shrimp!" said T. J., as Shrimp jumped for the bag. The boat rocked again.

I looked through the telescope. "There's two of them," I said. "And they're in a brand-new whaler. I think it's a Super Sport. Wow!"

It was the boat of my dreams. Don't get me wrong, I love the Captain's whaler, but it needs a lot of work. The paint is peeling, the hull is cracked, and the wheel is all rusty. It's from way back in the 1970s.

"Pirates?" asked T. J. He sadly watched Shrimp gulp down his jelly beans.

"Nah, it's Bryce and Trippy, I think."

"Yep," agreed Roger. "Bryce's dad told my mom all about Bryce's new whaler. He had it custom made and it's got a stereo and a GPS and special fishing rod thingies and cup holders. Bryce named it *The Viper*. Hiss!" Roger opened his mouth and stuck out his tongue as if he were a snake.

Roger's mom works as a real estate agent for Benedict Billings, the real estate king. He also happens to be Bryce and Beck's dad.

"Look at the babies playing pirates!" said Bryce as soon as he spotted us. He was wearing mirrored sunglasses, so we couldn't see his eyes.

"They're sure not going to get far in that beat-up old boat," said Trippy.

"Only babies play pirates," said Bryce.

"Who you calling babies?" I asked. Just because Bryce was eleven, that didn't mean he could talk to us like that.

"Yeah, we're pirates!" said Roger, who was still wearing his plastic teeth.

Bryce and Trippy laughed so hard, they doubled over.

"Oh, yeah?" I said before I could stop myself. "This may look like a game to you, but it's not. It's a training exercise."

"Huh?" said T. J. and Roger. They were both looking at me as if I had gone crazy.

"Training for what?" shot back Bryce. "To be pirates? I don't think so." He revved the whaler's awesome brand-new Mercury FourStroke engine.

"Later, babies," sneered Bryce.

"We're pirate hunters, actually," I said before I could stop myself. "Treasure hunters, to be exact." My eye fell on the plastic box of gold. "And we're . . . uh . . . looking for Captain Kidd's treasure."

Bryce and Trippy laughed at us.

"No one's ever found that treasure," said Bryce. "Not even real treasure hunters."

"That's right," chimed in Trippy.

"So, how are you going to find it?" asked Bryce.

Everyone's eyes were on me, even Shrimp's.

"He's just bluffing," said Bryce. "Why are we wasting our time talking to some dumb fourth-graders who don't even have a motor on their boat?!"

"I am not bluffing," I said. "We are *so* going to find it."

CAPTAIN KIDD (C. 1654-1701)

William Kidd, an excellent mariner, was hired by King William III of England to hunt down pirate ships and take their treasure. Some people thought he was a pirate, so he was put on trial in London. According to legend, he stopped at an island to bury his treasure before being captured in New York. He was hanged at Execution Dock in 1701.

"How?" asked Bryce. He sat back down and put his hands on the whaler's shiny silver wheel.

"Yeah, how?" asked T. J., staring at me with his mouth open so I could see all the chewed-up jelly beans.

"Maybe we know where Captain Kidd's treasure map is," I said. The words sprayed out of my mouth like water out of a whale's blowhole.

"No way!" said Bryce.

"That's for me to know and you to find out."

"I dare you, Fish Finelli!" Bryce laughed. "I double-doggie dare you to find that treasure. You're a big faker!"

"He is *not* a faker," said Roger and T. J.

"Let's see the map, then!" said Trippy.

"Yeah!" agreed Bryce, high-fiving him.

"It's not here," I said.

"Babies playing pirates is all you are." Bryce revved the motor again. "Yo-ho-ho!"

"Just you wait, Bryce! You'll see!"

"Oh, yeah?" shot back Bryce. "I bet you . . . " His voice trailed off as he frowned, thinking.

"Your sunglasses," Roger cut in. "Fish gets your sunglasses if he finds the treasure."

"Okay," said Bryce, his mirrored sunglasses catching the light as if they were on fire. I had to admit they were pretty cool. They were from Get Whooped, the surfer shop. And they were the kind real surfers wore.

"But if Bryce wins, what does he get?" said Trippy. "It's gotta be something good."

I looked at Roger. Roger looked at me. T. J. held up his almost empty box of Mallomars and shrugged.

"If I win—I mean *when* I win—Fish gives me fifty bucks," said Bryce. " 'Cause it's not like he has anything I'd ever want."

"Deal?" asked Trippy.

I didn't say anything for a minute. I was too busy thinking about how I had a whopping $27.51. How could I possibly give Bryce almost twice that? And forget about the Seagull. It would be long gone before I could even think about buying it.

"You know what you are?" said Bryce, revving the engine. He held up his forefinger and stuck out his thumb to make an L and pointed it right at me—the universal sign for loser.

The tips of my ears started burning, the way they do when I get really mad. "Deal," I said before I could think about it for one more second.

"You've got two weeks to get me my money," said Bryce. "Or you'll be sorry."

"You're the one who's going to be sorry when we find that treasure!" I shouted as the engine roared to life.

Bryce and Trippy shot off in a surge of spray that sent water all over us. Our boat rocked. Roger and T. J. looked at me as they wiped the water out of their eyes. Feenie and Mmm and Shrimp did, too. No one said anything for a long moment.

Then Roger grinned. "Fish, are you Captain Kidding me????!!!!"

THE LIBRARIAN'S GOT THE BOOTY?!

"It's very clear." Roger pointed to the gold-lettered sign. "By appointment only. And last time I checked, you did not have an appointment."

"What are we doing here?" asked T. J. He blew a big pink bubble with his gum. It popped all over his nose.

"T. J., can you quit chewing so loud?" I whispered. "We don't want anyone to notice us."

"Why not?" said T. J. "I brought my library card."

"I did, too," I said. "That's not the point."

"No, the point is, Fish, we need an appointment," said Roger. He made his *duh* face, which makes his eyes bulge like a squid's.

"Do you really think they'd give a kid an appointment?"

I shot back. "It says 'Researchers Must Go to the Front Desk for Assistance.' That means they'll know we're kids."

"So, what's the plan?" asked Roger.

"The Lioness donated a bunch of stuff to the library," I said. "So, maybe there's a map or a letter from when Captain Kidd landed on Lyons Island that will give us a clue."

The Lioness is what everybody calls Winthrop Lyons IV's widow, who lives on the island. She's supposed to be as tough as a lioness. That is pretty tough, since it's the females, not the males, who defend the pride.

"I'm starving," said T. J. He pulled a roll of SweeTarts out of his pocket and popped a fuzzy one into his mouth. It looked like it was covered with dryer lint.

Roger leaned against the door and put his ear to the shiny wood.

"Hear anything?" asked T. J.

Roger shook his head. "Silent as a dead man's chest. I say yo-ho-ho, let's go for it." He reached for the doorknob.

"Roger!" I hissed. "Don't!"

Suddenly, the knob started to turn all by itself.

We stepped back just as the door opened. A skinny woman with red-framed glasses stepped out. "Oh," she said in surprise. "Hello, gentlemen. Sorry, but I've got to run. I'll be back in fifteen minutes." She hurried down the hall, as Roger put his foot in the space between the door and the jamb so it wouldn't lock.

"Fifteen minutes, Finelli. Ready, set, go!" Roger took his foot out of the doorframe. "The usual warning if there's trouble, okay?"

Heart pounding, I slipped inside. There were old wooden bookcases filled with old leather-bound books. Under the window was a desk with a computer on it. Opposite that was a long, glass-covered table.

I went over to take a look. Under the glass was a whale jawbone with a scrimshaw design of a ship, a beat-up arrowhead, and an old map. Maybe it was a treasure map! I looked closer. Nope. It was just a map of the town.

"Now what?" I said.

I turned. My eye was caught by the letters on the cabinet drawer in front of me. It read *AB–AS*. The one below read *AT–BD*.

The card catalog! Perfect! Instead of computers, libraries used to have these cabinets with cards in them, called card catalogs. Each card lists the name of a book, its author, and some stuff about it. Each book also has a call number that tells you where to find it. It's called the Dewey Decimal System 'cause it was invented by this dude, Melvil Dewey, back in the 1800s. And lots of the call numbers have decimal points. Dewey Decimal—get it? I could look up Captain Kidd and find the call numbers for the books about him.

I reached for the *C* drawer. Then I remembered that it wasn't like Captain was Captain Kidd's first name. That was William. I was just bending down for the *WA–WU* drawer when I realized that stuff is usually alphabetized by last name, not first. So I needed a *K* drawer. As I scanned for *K*, I spotted the words *Lyons Island* on one whole drawer. *Sweet!*

I flipped through cards about the island's ecosystems. Next was a bunch of cards about Winthrop Lyons and the Native American chief who gave him the island in the first place. Turns out it was called Monchonake (*mahn-cho-nake*) back then, which means Island of Death. Spooky.

And then I came to one card that read in this teensy, old-fashioned writing: *A List of the Treasure Left by Capn. W. K. to W. Lyons, including Pieces of Eight, Arabian gold, emeralds, rubies, diamonds . . .*

PIECES OF EIGHT

Also known as Spanish dollars, they were first minted in 1497 in Spain. Each was worth eight reales (see why it's called a piece of eight?). The first United States silver dollar was based on it, although the dollar contained less silver than a piece of eight and so was really worth less.

Just then a deep voice out in the hall said, "Boys, may I help you?"

I froze.

"Um . . . no . . . thank you, Mystery—I mean, Mr. Mann," said Roger in his serious voice. Mr. E. Mann is the director of the Whooping Hollow Library. No one knows what the *E* actually stands for— it's a mystery (get it?). A lot of the kids call him Mystery Man and think he's a spy. He is pretty cool. He's traveled all over the world. He wears black clothes, and they say he has a pair of night-vision goggles in his briefcase and poison darts in the tips of his shiny leather shoes. He drives a superfast silver sports car and he can raise one eyebrow.

"We were just doing research for a report," Roger said. "You know, for school."

"That's strange, since school is out for the summer."

Mystery Man had a point there.

"It's . . . um, summer homework . . . you know, to keep

our minds busy, so they don't dry up," said Roger.

"What is the topic of this report that requires you to be in this particular section of the library?" Mystery Man asked in his deep voice. I bet he was arching his eyebrow, too.

"Funny you should ask," began Roger.

"Since you do not appear to have an answer at the present moment, perhaps you would like to return when you do. *Ciao!*"

Mystery Man might not be a spy, but he sure was cool. *Ciao* means "good-bye" in Italian, by the way.

TAP! TAP! I heard footsteps moving down the hall.

"Seagulls don't eat ice cream!" shouted T. J. "Seagulls don't wear sneakers. Seagulls don't—"

"SEAGULLS DON'T EAT PICKLES!" Roger yelled at the top of his lungs.

OH, NO! Our secret password!

My eyes darted wildly around the room, searching for an escape hatch. I heard the sound of a key in the lock. Then the doorknob began to turn.

Mystery Man stuck one foot in the room. I dove for the only cover I could find—the desk. I sure hoped he wasn't planning to sit down, or I would be as doomed as a night crawler on the end of a fishing hook.

I watched as Mystery Man's shiny, pointy shoes headed my way. I closed my eyes and took a deep breath. When I opened them again, the shoes were just in front of me. What was Mystery Man doing? A minute passed, and then another. I started sweating. If he moved one inch closer, he'd step on me.

Just then Mystery Man cleared his throat like he was coughing up a humongous clam. He started talking in this weird, low voice. I had to strain my ears to hear him.

" . . . *mumble* . . . lost treasure . . . the map . . . *mumble* . . ."

Treasure map??? There was a pause.

"Pirates . . . *mumble* . . ." I held my breath, listening. "W. K. . . . "

My mind started racing. Pirates? Map? W. K. as in—it couldn't be, but then again, what else could it be but CAPTAIN WILLIAM KIDD????!!!

Mystery Man's voice dropped to an even lower whisper. "Seven-thirty. At the duck pond . . . treasure . . . "

Just then an incredibly loud, pulsing buzz filled the air. BUZZ! BUZZ! BUZZ! BUZZ!

I was so startled I almost grabbed one of Mystery Man's poison-dart shoes. Even worse, I couldn't hear the end of what he said. Something about treasure, but what did that have to do with the duck pond? Was he planning to hunt for Captain Kidd's treasure at the duck pond?

The alarm kept ringing and Mystery Man's shiny poison-dart shoes left the room. I counted to sixty hippopotamus. I figured by then it would be safe to come out.

When I reached the hallway, Roger and T. J. were nowhere to be seen. There was nobody around at all. I raced out the door.

"Over here, Fish!" they called. They were standing in the parking lot.

"Phew!" I said. "That was a close one!"

"You're telling me," said Roger. "Lucky for you it was fire drill time." He winked.

"You didn't—" I began.

Roger drew his finger across his lips like he was zipping up a zipper.

I shook my head. Roger was always goofing around. He might have pulled the fire alarm, but then again he might not have. There was no way to tell. And that was just the way he liked it.

"So, did you find the treasure map?" T. J. asked.

"No, but you'll never guess who else is hunting for Captain Kidd's treasure . . . "

"Who?" asked T. J.

Before I could answer, Mystery Man came walking across the parking lot. He was with the librarian with the red glasses. He wasn't arching one eyebrow and making his "I'm a supercool undercover operative" face. He was smiling at her. It was like seeing a bluefish blow you a kiss instead of bite your finger off when it was on the end of your line.

I nodded at Mystery Man.

"What the heck?!" said Roger.

"Yep! It's Mystery Man and I'm pretty sure he has the treasure map."

"Whoa!" said Roger. "The librarian's got the booty!"

OPERATION QUACK

"We've got to figure out what Mystery Man is up to," I said, as I carefully pushed my way through the last of the pricker bushes.

"Ouch!" said T. J. behind me.

"Faster, Mahoney!" said Roger. "If you quadruple your speed, you won't get pricked."

OOMPH! T. J. knocked into me as Roger knocked into him.

The three of us fell into a pile in the middle of the Monkey Fort. Big tupelo trees surrounded us. Their branches twisted together over our heads so it was like being in a tent. No one knows about the Monkey Fort except for us, maybe because of the pricker bushes. It's where we hold our top-secret meetings.

"If Mystery Man has the map, it's only logical he must be planning to dig up the treasure." I stood up and started to pace.

"I sure got pricked." T. J. pulled some prickers out of his arm. "I'm telling you, speed's got nothing to do with it."

"Does so," said Roger. "It's how fast you—"

"Your shorts are ripped again," interrupted T. J., pointing to the jagged hole in the knee of Roger's cargo shorts. "That's 'cause of the prickers, so—"

"Guys, let's review the facts from the top," I said.

Roger jumped up and grabbed a stick. He drew two circles in the dirt. He wrote the letters *W* and *K* in one circle, and put a big blob with two smaller blobs under it and the number 730 in the other, diagramming the evidence.

"Whar doze bwahs?" T. J. asked, his mouth full of Tootsie Roll.

"Those aren't blobs," said Roger. "I diagrammed the evidence. That is a mama duck and two baby ducks. You knew those were ducks, right, Fish?"

"Yes! No! I mean, your drawing skills are not the point right now, Roger. We need to figure out why Mystery Man is secretly meeting someone about Captain Kidd's treasure tonight at seven-thirty at the duck pond."

"If I had the map, I'd just start digging," said T. J. He reached under the branch he was sitting on and pulled out the cooler. There was nothing in it except an almost empty bottle of Yoo-hoo that some ants were crawling around on.

"There must be a reason he can't," I said, "which is why he's having the meeting at the duck pond in the first place."

Roger raised his eyebrows at me. "Are you thinking what I'm thinking?"

"No way."

"Way."

"What are you guys talking about?" asked T. J., his eyes on the Yoo-hoo.

"It's too risky. We might get caught," I said.

"Not if we go undercover," said Roger.

"As what?" I asked. "Ducks?"

"Nah," said Roger. "As trees. T. J. can get his dad's camo face paint. Hunting season's over, so he won't miss it, right, T. J.?"

"I guess, but what do we want to be trees for?"

"We're not going to really *be* trees, T. J.," explained Roger. "We're going to camouflage ourselves so that we blend in with the trees."

"Oh, I get it. Why?"

"So nobody sees us."

"Are you sure that's a good idea?" asked T. J. He brushed the ants off the Yoo-hoo bottle and took a long swig.

"Chocolate-covered ants—yummy, dude!" said Roger.

T. J. shrugged and burped "delicious." He can actually burp whole sentences. Once at school he burped the entire Pledge of Allegiance.

"We don't have a choice," I said. "We *have* to. This isn't just about the bet anymore. It's our duty to make sure Mystery Man and his partner don't steal the treasure. We have to protect it in the name of the Lioness and the town of Whooping Hollow and the government of the United States."

"Yeah!" yelled Roger. "For the Lioness and the town of Whooping Hollow and the government of the United States!"

"We'll show him and stinky old Bryce, too," I added.

"Hey," said Roger. "Maybe Mystery Man is a double agent for another country and posing as a spy for our country, whose cover is that he's the director of the Whooping Hollow Library."

"You know what, Rog?" I shook my head. "You watch way too much TV."

"I'm just saying," said Roger. "It could explain a lot, like why he's got the poison darts in his shoes. If someone blows his cover, he can shoot them to silence them."

"Whoa!" said T. J. "We better tell Officer Babinski about this, since he's the chief of police."

"We can't," I said. "Remember? I wasn't supposed to be in the Special Collection in the first place. And in the second place, Roger's just making up that double agent stuff. And in the third place, it's no crime for someone to meet someone else at the duck pond."

"Then what are we going there for?"

"We're going because we're trying to prevent a crime from happening."

"Oh, I get it," said T. J. "Kinda like Batman and Robin."

"Exactly," I said.

"Bring some of your dad's hunting clothes, too, T. J.," said Roger. "You know, camo hats and shirts and stuff."

T. J. frowned. "Okay, but I get first dibs on the duck whistle, since it's my dad's."

"Quack! Quack!" Roger and I said.

"Quack! Quack!" T. J. chimed in.

"Every mission needs a name," said Roger after we stopped quacking. "Let's call it . . . Operation Quack!"

QUACKERJACKS!

It was going to be a perfect night for a stakeout—warm but not too hot. The sky was blue, with just a few pink clouds. And there was a sliver of moon in the sky.

I knocked on Roger's back door.

"Password?"

"Roger, it's me," I said. "Let me in."

"Password."

"Come on, Roger. We don't have time."

"I'll give you a hint. It rhymes with *tack*."

I rolled my eyes. "Quack!"

The door opened. Roger was wearing a camo fishing hat and a gigantic pair of hip waders. He had a garden hose tied around his waist to hold them up.

I laughed. "How are you going to walk in those?"

"Whaddya mean?" asked Roger, just as he tripped and landed on the kitchen floor. "A little practice is all I need."

"Where's Summer?" I said as we headed down the basement steps.

Roger pointed his finger up. "On the phone with the BFFs."

I smiled. That was why we were meeting at Roger's house. His mom was working late and Summer was in charge. That meant as long as the house didn't burn down, Roger could pretty much do what he wanted.

T. J. was reading one of Roger's vampire comic books. He was wearing a camo fleece and baseball cap, and was sucking down a cherry Pixy Stix. Roger tossed me a camo thermal.

"Let's go, guys," I said.

"Hold up, Finelli," said Roger. "We need to do an equipment check." He peered at a piece of paper that looked a lot like an old math test. Roger's really good in math, but he hates to show his work, so the teacher puts red frowny faces next to his answers.

"Binocs?" he asked.

"Check." I pulled a pair of binoculars out of my backpack.

"Rope?"

"Check." I waved the rope around.

"Flashlight? Wait! I've got that." Roger dug around in the Bug Patrol backpack. "Ta-da!" He pulled out a pink Barbie flashlight.

When we finished going over our equipment, T. J. jumped up. "Guys, you forgot the most important thing—snacks!" He tossed us each a Blow Pop.

"Now for the final touch," said Roger. He opened a tin of dark, goopy stuff. "Fish, you're the first victim."

Before I could react, Roger smeared some all over my face. It was cold and gooey and smelled like skunk and toothpaste. YUCK!

When we were finally all face-painted, we headed up the steps and outside. I could hear the mower in my yard, which meant my mom and dad were still gardening.

I sure hoped Mystery Man and his partner would be punctual. If I wasn't home by dark, I would be grounded for sure. Fortunately, sunset would be at 8:07 tonight. That meant it wouldn't be dark till close to nine.

"Don't you have to tell Summer you're leaving?" T. J. asked, blowing a big pink bubble. T. J. can demolish a Blow Pop faster than an octopus can suck up a clam.

"Summer!" shouted Roger.

"Not so loud!" I grabbed Roger's arm and pointed toward my yard.

"Carmine!" we heard my mother. "The petunias!"

My dad loves to pretend he's going to mow over my mom's flowers. Even though he never does, my mom falls for it every time.

Roger picked up a pebble and tossed it at Summer's window. He missed. He threw another rock. This one hit the glass. PLINK!

Seconds later, Summer stuck her head out the window. "Roger, is that you?" she yelled.

Roger put his finger to his lips.

"Roger?!" Summer was staring straight down at us, but it was like we were invisible.

"Whatever!!!" With a disgusted sigh, she banged the window shut.

"I told you this camo would work," said Roger. He bumped one shoulder into me and the other into T. J. "It's the perfect cover."

The duck pond is only a few blocks from our houses. We got there just as the sun was beginning to set. The place was full of quiet shadows from the tall, old trees.

Now that it's summertime, the geese have moved in. Geese aren't the nicest waterfowl, so you don't want to make them mad. But what you really have to remember is to watch your step, so you don't wind up with slimy, disgusting goose poop stuck to your shoes.

You also have to beware of the mutants. They're these weird creatures that are part duck, part goose, part swan, and totally mean. No one knows where they came from. They say a mutant can bite off a kid's hand with just one chomp of its razor-sharp beak.

"Now what?" asked Roger.

I stared around at all the trees and the darkened trails leading off in different directions. We would have to spread out. I reached into my pocket and pulled out my compass.

"Roger, you go east," I said. "T. J., you go west, and I'll go north."

T. J. chomped on a handful of Cracker Jack. "Hey, you forgot south."

"No, I didn't. The entrance to the duck pond is our point of origin, so the only thing south of us is Main Street."

"Better stay in radio contact," added Roger. "Right, Marco Polo, O great explorer who discovered India—"

"That was Vasco da Gama," I cut in.

**MARCO POLO
(C. 1254-1324)**

Marco Polo was an Italian merchant and explorer. He was one of the first travelers to go all the way from Europe to China. When he returned to Venice 24 years later, he wrote about what he had seen and learned.

"Fish!"

"I can't help it if Marco Polo went to China, not India."

"The point is," continued Roger, "whoever spots the suspects should alert the other members of the team."

We pulled out our walkie-talkies and flipped the switches to ON.

"Hey, what about me?" said T. J., pieces of Cracker Jack shooting out of his mouth.

Roger's eyes lit up. "I know. Blow the duck whistle. You've got it, right?"

T. J. nodded and pulled out the yellow plastic whistle. It looked kinda like a kazoo.

"Just blow it if you see Mystery Man and we'll come," I said. Then I handed T. J. my clipboard and pen. "Here. Write down everything you hear. It's important, okay?"

T. J. nodded. He bent his head over the clipboard and started to write.

"What are you writing?" I asked.

"Everything you said," said T. J.

"You're not supposed to write what *I* say."

"But you said to write everything important. And what you said is important, right?"

"No," I began.

"But you said it was."

"Yes, it is, but that's not . . . "

Roger and T. J. laughed. "T. J. got you good," Roger said.

T. J. winked at me. I shook my head, but I had to admit it: He got me. T. J. is way smarter than he sometimes acts.

"Time to move out, men!" said Roger. He held up a hand, pinky out. T. J. and I held ours out, too. We all hooked pinkies. Then we did our secret handshake. And said our secret password: "S.D.E.P." And we bumped fists again.

In case you were wondering, S.D.E.P. stands for "Seagulls Don't Eat Pickles." It's been our password since second grade, after Summer got mad at Roger and told everyone in school our old password. Okay, I'll tell you, too—it was A.N.T. (Alien Ninja Turkeys—I know, totally lame, but we were little kids.)

I headed down the main trail. I tried to walk quietly, but every twig that crunched sounded as loud as my Uncle

Norman's motorcycle when it backfires. I kept glancing over my shoulder, but there was no one there. I walked over a footbridge. On the other side were some benches. A perfect spot for a clandestine (*spy word for secret*) meeting. I crouched behind a bush. Then I moved slowly toward the clearing.

I stopped and listened. I didn't hear anything except the pounding of my own heart. And when I looked up, there was no one there, not even a duck.

I recrossed the bridge back to the main trail. I was about to take the path to the right when my walkie-talkie crackled.

"Mayday! Mayday!" came Roger's staticky voice. "They've got me surrounded! There's no way out!"

DUCK, DUCK, GOOSE-POOPED!

"Roger!" I said into my walkie-talkie. There was no answer.

"Roger!"

"Sorry," said Roger. "My walkie-talkie got pooped."

"Ew!" Goose poop seriously puts the *N* in nasty.

"Listen, Fish, I need help A.S.A.P. They won't leave me alone. And they look real hungry."

He couldn't mean Mystery Man and his partner—or could he? But hungry for what? Roger? No way. Mystery Man might be a spy, but he was no cannibal. "Who?"

"Get away from me!"

"Who has you surrounded? Who looks hungry?" I yelled into the walkie-talkie.

Seconds passed. And then, "The mutants."

Oh, no! The mutants. Roger's hand was going to be chomped off. His blood and guts would be scattered all over. I had to help him!

"Where are you?"

There was no answer. Just static.

"Roger!"

Still nothing. I didn't know if I was sweating from panic or from T. J.'s dad's camo gear.

I turned back the way I had come. If Roger was somewhere east, that would be to my left, since now I was going south instead of north.

"Roger, can you give me your coordinates?" I asked.

Nothing.

I hurried along, hoping Roger was okay. I was just rounding the next bend when I heard a rustling sound. I paused, listening.

SWISH! THUD! SWISH! THUD!

Someone was walking down the path just across from me. I couldn't see who it was unless I crossed over the central trail. If I did, I would be changing course and going west when Roger was somewhere in the opposite direction. It would just take a minute.

I darted across the trail. SWOOSH! THUD! I hunkered down so my head was level with the duckweed. I crawl-walked forward. I couldn't see anyone, but the footsteps were getting closer.

I hurried around the next bend and ducked behind a beech tree. *Aha!* There was someone in the shadows. I pulled out the binoculars to get a better look, but they didn't help. Whoever it was just looked like a bigger black blob. Something about the bulky shape made me think it was a man, though. He was definitely slowing down. He seemed to be heading for the bench just over the bridge.

SQUISH! SWOOSH! SQUISH!

The man stopped suddenly. "*Zut!*" exclaimed a deep voice.

My eyes almost popped out of my head. I knew that deep voice. It belonged to Mystery Man. And even though I didn't know what *Zut* meant, it sounded like some cool foreign word you would say if you had just been pooped. I guess no one told him about the geese.

Mystery Man knocked his pooped shoe against a tree, but goose poop has similar properties to rubber cement. The more you rub it, the more it sticks. He started hopping around to try to get it off. I had to hold my breath so I wouldn't laugh.

"Of all the vile substances," I heard Mystery Man angrily mutter.

A minute later, he headed across the bridge. I waited until he sat down on the bench. I inched my way after him. I noticed there was a tree behind the bench and wondered if I could hide behind it.

I was staring at the tree when my eye was caught by something white. I squinted. That's when I saw there was a hand holding the white thing. The hand belonged to a person who was sitting in the tree. I blinked and looked again, but how many red-headed boys could there be at the duck pond at 7:30 at night?

It was T. J. all right! The white thing was the paper in the clipboard.

I edged closer and stopped right by the bridge. Just then Mystery Man stood and waved to someone out of sight on the other side of the tree. I had a feeling it was his partner! *Oh, man!*

At that moment, my walkie-talkie crackled to life. "Abort mission! Do you read?" said Roger.

I ducked down so the grass would muffle the sound.

"Read and copy," I said. There was no time to ask how he'd gotten rid of the mutants. I was just glad he was okay. I whispered to him what was going on, and gave him directions.

I had to figure out how to get to the tree before T. J. blew the duck whistle. If he did, I was afraid Mystery Man would look up and see him.

I lay down on my belly and inched along the muddy trail. I was eyeball to eyeball with goose poop. It was everywhere. Poop smooshed under my legs and arms. Some even got on my nose. The smell was so bad, I gagged.

I could feel the hot dogs and beans I had for dinner on their way back up. I swallowed hard.

EMU

The emu is the largest bird native to Australia. It is brown and flightless and stands up to 6½ feet tall.

"Did you see that?" Mystery Man said. "There's an animal on the bridge."

My heart started pounding. I lay still, trying not to breathe.

"No, it was much bigger than a duck," he went on. "It was the size of an emu."

I lifted my head slowly. Mystery Man was still standing and staring my way.

Uh-oh! I had to hide. But where? I couldn't get up and sprint for the trees. They would see me for sure.

That left only one option—the water. The mucky, yucky to the millionth degree water. I held my nose, and slid off the bridge and into the pond. If getting pooped was 9¾ on a scale of 1 to 10 of nasty, wading through the pond was 10 to the 10th power (*10 billion, in case you don't know how to calculate exponents*).

Slimy stuff coated my legs and arms. I tried hard not to think of just how many ducks had been you-know-what'ing in the water. Plus, there were the moldy scraps of bread that floated by and all the pond scum.

When I reached the other side, I pulled myself up. I took a deep breath of fresh air. *Phew!*

Mystery Man was sitting down again, looking the other way. I scrambled up the bank. Then I crouched down and began to work my way to the tree, my eyes on Mystery Man.

I was halfway there when he suddenly stood up. He handed something to his partner. Something flat and rectangular. The map! It had to be! If only I could hear what they were saying. I sure hoped T. J. was taking good notes.

I was almost at the tree and I just had to signal T. J. I looked up and saw a flash of white. T. J. was moving his arm. He was holding something up to his mouth. *Oh, no!* It was the duck whistle.

I had to stop him. I stood up and waved my arms. Then I ducked back down so Mystery Man wouldn't see me.

Don't blow it! I thought hard at T. J. But it was no use. The next instant the loudest-ever QUACK-QUACK-QUACKING filled the air. The sound of flapping wings and the calls of hundreds of ducks echoed through the trees. Ducks flew, swam, and swarmed to our part of the pond. Water churned. Feathers flew. It must have been the party call, because I've never seen so many ducks in one place in my life.

It was the end of our stakeout. Mystery Man and his partner hurried off. They had to leave; with all the noise and approaching ducks, no one could hear themselves think, let alone talk. They fled west, so I never even got a tiny peek at his partner.

"Hey," said Roger, coming up behind me. "What's going on?"

I nodded my head at the tree. "T. J. blew the duck whistle."

"Wow!" said T. J., landing with a thud beside us. "The package said it was the feeding call. Guess those ducks were hungry for a midnight snack."

I sighed. "Well, this stakeout sure stank."

"Not as much as you do, dude," said Roger. He held his nose as he stared at me.

"Yeah, Fish, what happened to you?" said T. J.

I glared at both of them as I tried to wring the water out of Mr. Mahoney's dripping-wet thermal. "Will you guys knock it off?! Way worse than how I smell is how messed up this stakeout was."

"Whaddya mean?" said T. J. "I wrote down all the important stuff, just like you told me."

"You did?" I said in surprise. "Let me see."

T. J. handed me the clipboard. There were tic-tac-toe games all over the page.

"What does tic-tac-toe have to do with anything?"

"Sorry. Wrong page. I won every game, in case you were wondering." T. J. grinned and grabbed back the clipboard. He flipped the pages.

T. J. had drawn a jaggedy circle with a square in the middle. There was a skull and crossbones on top of the square. And the only two words he had written made no sense at all . . . MUNCH EGGS.

"Munch eggs?! What does that mean?"

"Scrambled, sunny-side up, hard-boiled, fried," joked Roger. "Just a few of the many ways I like to munch my eggs. Oh, and how could I forget my favorite—egg salad."

"T. J., what's this about?" I asked.

"Simple. Mystery Man is looking for a treasure chest with a skull and crossbones on it that's on some island called Munch Eggs. I thought I drew the island pretty good."

"Whoever heard of an island called Munch Eggs?"

"EGG-zactly what I was wondering," put in Roger with a grin.

"Egg-zactly!" repeated T. J. "That's funny. Eggs. Egg-zactly. I get it."

"I don't!" I said. "There is nothing to get, since eggs have nothing to do with anything. I bet you heard wrong. Munch Eggs can't be the name of the island. Think, T. J. Are you sure that's what you heard?"

T. J. popped a handful of Sugar Babies in his mouth. It took him what felt like forever to chew them. "Uh-huh," he finally said.

"Who's Mystery Man's partner?" I asked. "Did you get a good look?"

We both stared hard at T. J. He shrugged again and kept munching. "I dunno. He spoke real soft."

"Okay, but what does he look like?"

"I only saw his fingers. They were skinny, and one had a big red ring on it that looked kinda like a mood ring. I think when the ring turns red it means love or—"

"Skinny fingers and a mood ring???!!!"

T. J. popped some more Sugar Babies in his mouth and nodded.

"So what did Mystery Man say when he showed his partner the map?" I asked.

"What map?"

"The treasure map."

"He didn't give him a map," said T. J. "Just candy."

"Candy?!"

"Yeah, I'm pretty sure it was a box of those chocolates in the wrappers that have all different fillings. I like the ones with nuts, except for almonds, and the cherry ones are sorta squishy, but—"

"T. J., that makes no sense. Treasure hunters do not give each other chocolate."

"Eggs and chocolate," said Roger. "Now there's a new breakfast combo."

"T. J., all you ever think about is food. Do you remember anything else they said? Anything to do with the treasure or the island or the map?"

T. J. poured the last of the box of Cracker Jack into his mouth. Suddenly, his eyes lit up. "The map! It's in the treasure chest!"

"T. J., that can't be right. Who puts a treasure map in a treasure chest? That's where the treasure goes," I said.

Just then a whip-poor-will gave the strange, whooping call they're named for. They're nocturnal, and the cry they make is pretty creepy. I can understand why Native Americans thought they were birds of death. All three of us jumped.

"Uh-oh, guys, it's almost dark," said T. J.

"Run!" said Roger.

The three of us ran as fast as we could until Roger's waders fell down. Then we had to take turns helping to hold them up. See, Roger had left his hose belt behind with the mutants. It's what he used to make his getaway. It turns out hoses totally terrify them.

By the time I got to my house, it was dark. That meant I was late. I slunk around back, where the old apple tree goes up to my window. I climbed as fast as I could and slowly opened the window so it wouldn't creak.

"Fish! It's bedtime!" my mom yelled up the stairs.

"Okay, Mom!"

I jumped off the window ledge into my room, pulled off my pooped clothes, and put on my pajamas. I was safe!

"Where have you been?" Feenie asked, barging into my room.

"You're supposed to knock," I said. I kicked my pooped clothes under the bed.

Feenie wrinkled her nose. "Something smells in here. Like—"

"A FAPIT like you needs her beauty sleep." I pushed her out the door.

"I know you're up to something, Fish Finelli," she said. "How come your face is all dirty?"

Oops! I forgot about the camo face paint.

"It has to do with that boy Bryce and that kid's treasure. Right?"

I gulped, but didn't say anything. Feenie is only four and a half. Her mind is like a steel trap.

"Nighty-night," I said, closing my door. "Sleep tight."

"I know I'm right," Feenie shouted from the other side.

"Don't let the bedbugs bite!" I yelled back.

"Right about what?" Mom asked.

I held my breath, wondering if Feenie would tell.

"It's private, Mom," Feenie finally said. "You know, brother-sister stuff."

I smiled and lay down on my bed. Before I knew it, I was fast asleep. I sure was *pooped*—if you know what I mean.

EGG-ZACTLY!

"Her name is Venus Star," said my mom. "So you should call her Ms. Star."

"That's a weird name," I said, "since Venus isn't a star, it's a planet."

Uncle Norman was bringing his latest girlfriend over for dinner. She's an astrologer. That's someone who figures out how the stars affect us here on Earth.

"Fish, please take the potatoes out to the grill," said my mom. All of her attention was focused on the double boiler. She was melting chocolate for a dessert with a fancy French name that looked a lot like brownies.

It had been a week since our stakeout. And none of us could figure out where in the heck Munch Eggs Island might be. I still thought T. J. heard wrong and it didn't even exist.

On top of that, there were only five days left until the bet was up. Then I would have to pay Bryce the fifty bucks. I didn't want to admit it, but Bryce was right. I had no clue how to find Captain Kidd's treasure.

Just then I heard the POP! POP! POP! of Uncle Norman's motorcycle backfiring. Shrimp started barking and ran out the door.

"Uncle Norman!" came Feenie's voice. "See my wings! I'm a FAPIT!"

A few minutes later, Uncle Norman walked into the kitchen with a woman in a long, green, sparkly dress. She shook my hand and smiled.

"You have a very powerful aura, Norman. It's blue and green. Blue for wisdom, and green for making things happen. So pleased to meet you." Her eyes sparkled like her dress.

"Venus says everyone's got an aura," said Uncle Norman. He put his arm around her. *Oh, man!* Doing the arm thing meant only one thing—he was serious about her, all right.

Feenie raced over just then, waving her magic wand. "Want me to make magic for you?"

Uncle Norman grinned and threw Feenie up in the air.

We all headed out to the backyard. Feenie started doing magic tricks with her wand. She made Shrimp lie down and roll over and sit up. They were all commands I had taught him, and had zero to do with magic. Venus clapped and so did Uncle Norman, even though he's seen Feenie do this routine a million times.

I put the potatoes on the picnic table. A second later, Roger's head popped up over the hedge.

"Hungry, Roger?" asked my dad. He speared a potato with his barbecue fork. He was wearing his favorite barbecue apron that reads *Plumbers like it PIPING hot!* There's a picture of a flaming pipe in a giant hot dog bun on the chest.

"What's for dinner?" Roger wanted to know.

"The striped bass Uncle Norman caught," I said.

"Grilled with a light layer of lemon and a tad of butter like usual? I'm in," said Roger. He disappeared into the hedge.

My dad grinned and turned the potatoes on the grill.

"Fish, time to set the table!" called my mom.

"Coming!" I said, just as Roger reappeared at the end of the yard where our secret passage comes out.

"Last one there's a rotten egg!" said Roger, running past me.

I took off. I was just passing him when he elbowed me. He touched the screen door first.

"Beat ya, rotten egg!" said Roger.

"Cheater," I said.

I handed him the big plate with the fish and picked up the silverware and napkins.

"Oh, and throw away this newspaper," my mom said, wrinkling her nose. She handed me the newspaper Uncle Norman had used to wrap up the fish.

On our way across the yard, Dude started winding himself around our legs. He was purring as loud as a washing machine. Fish is number one on his favorite food list. He jumped up in the air, trying to reach the plate with the fish.

"Kitty cat want the fishy?" Roger teased. He held the plate down lower.

Dude jumped. Roger barely got the fish away in time.

"Dude, you're one fast dude!" said Roger.

"I'll take that," said my dad. He had seen Dude nab a fish faster than you can say holy mackerel!

I threw the paper in the garbage can. We were just

sitting down to eat when there was a loud CRASH. Seconds later, Dude raced across the grass, batting the fishy newspaper between his paws. Shrimp barked and ran after him.

"Bad kitty cat!" yelled Feenie. "Bad doggie!"

"Wow!" said Roger. "That Dude is one determined dude."

"I wouldn't be surprised if he were a Capricorn," remarked Venus Star. "They tend to be quite goal-oriented. Is his birthday in December or January?" She smiled at my mom.

"I . . . don't . . . know exactly. We found him on the porch one day," said my mom. She was blinking a lot, the way she does when she doesn't know what to say.

"I don't normally cast horoscopes for animals, but I know other astrologers who do."

My mom's blinking turned into mad eyelash batting. Behind us, Dude yowled as Shrimp pulled the newspaper from him.

"Fish, will you throw away that paper, please?!" asked my mom.

"No problem, Mrs. F.," said Roger, jumping up.

I sighed and got up, too.

Roger and I reached for the paper at the same time. It ripped in half. I was wadding up my half when my

eye caught the headline: LAST ROAR FOR LYONS ISLAND!

"Hey, Rog, lemme see your half!"

I brushed off the gooey fish gunk and read:

"Eugenia Lyons, wife of the late Winthrop Lyons, may be forced to sell Lyons Island, as its upkeep as a nature preserve has become too costly. The state will only supply funds if it is declared a historic landmark. Stories abound of the burial of pirate treasure there by the notorious Captain Kidd, but such treasure has never been found. Some claim he hid a treasure map in a trunk with—"

That was it. Uncle Norman must have thrown away the rest of the paper.

"Who would buy Lyons Island?" I asked.

Roger rubbed his fingers together. "Someone with mucho dough."

I raised an eyebrow.

"You know—benjamins, moolah, cash. You get my drift."

I sighed as we sat back down. "I know dough is money. The question is, will the Lioness really sell Lyons Island?"

All the adults looked up at my question.

"She'll have to," said Uncle Norman. "Unless it's confirmed as a landmark. Then the state will fund its upkeep."

Uncle Norman knows a lot about land. He worked for a surveyor, like, a million years ago. That was before he was captain of a yacht, head of a lobster boat in Central America, and a rock star. He finally wound up becoming a plumber like my dad.

"I heard she's having a garden party to prove her case to the mayor," said my mom. "And an expert on the history of the island is going to speak."

"Lyons Island," said Venus in a dreamy voice. Her eyes had a faraway look. "Strange."

"What's strange?" Uncle Norman asked.

"Something I saw when I was there. It's just coming back to me now."

"You went to Lyons Island?" I asked. It wasn't like anyone could just go there. You had to be invited.

Venus blinked and nodded. "Once, a long time ago."

"What did you see?" asked Roger.

Venus's eyes got that faraway look again. "An old map, like a treasure map, with an island in the middle of it."

Roger and I looked at each other. "Map?" he mouthed.

"And there was a chest," she went on. "One of those old-fashioned ones with an iron padlock that sailors used to take to sea."

"Like a treasure chest?" I said, my heart beating faster. Venus nodded.

"So, where was the map?" I asked.

"Oh, I don't know," said Venus. "I saw it in a vision as I was walking through the house."

"A vision?" repeated my mother, her eyebrows shooting up again.

"I sure hope Mrs. Lyons doesn't have to sell the island," Uncle Norman said, after a quick glance at my mom. "It's almost the same as it was when Chief Wyandanch gave it to the first Lyons almost four hundred years ago. It was called something different then, of course."

"Yes," agreed Venus. "The Native Americans gave the land such beautiful names. It started with an *M*, I think."

I was about to ask about the map again when I realized she was right. I remembered reading the Native American name of the island when I was in the library. It had something to do with death. And it did begin with an *M*. What was it? It seemed very important to remember.

"Murdo . . . " I began. "Monko . . . Muncho . . . " My eyes opened wide as it hit me."Munch Eggs!"

Everyone stared at me. Roger started to grin.

"T. J. was right! He said it was called Munch Eggs. But it was really called Monchonake."

"Monchonake," agreed Venus.

"You know what Monchonake sounds like?" I said.

"Munch Eggs!" Roger jumped up to high-five me.

"Egg-zactly!"

SEAGULLS DON'T EAT PICKLES

"Remind me why we're going to Lyons Island?" asked T. J.

It was the next morning, and I had called the guys over for an emergency meeting.

"We're going because that's where the treasure map is," I said. "And the treasure, too, I bet. You were right all along."

"You can say that again," said T. J., grinning.

"That," said Roger.

T. J. threw a malt ball at him. Roger ducked, and Shrimp opened his jaws and caught it. Then he swallowed it, closed his eyes, and went back to sleep.

"We have to figure out a way to get there before Mystery Man and his partner do," I said.

"You mean trespass," said Roger, "since last time I checked, no one was allowed to go to Lyons Island without an invite."

"What about the man-eating alligator that guards the place and the lion in the basement?" asked T. J. in a low voice. "Mickey told me—"

"When was the last time you saw an alligator outside an aquarium, T. J.?" I asked. "That's just a made-up story to scare kids away. Alligators can't live in water as cold as the Atlantic Ocean. And lions need to live in a hot, dry climate like Africa."

Just then a siren started to sound from inside my house. T. J. and Roger looked at me.

"Dude, what was that?!"

"Finelli & Finelli's Plumbing and Heating emergency hotline," I said. "Now listen. We've got to figure out how to get a boat quick. If only I had the Seagull . . ."

T. J.'s watch buzzed all of a sudden. "Gotta go!"

We stared at him in surprise. T. J. is never in a hurry for anything. "What's the big rush?" I asked.

"Pancakes. I don't want to be late, or Mickey and Mmm will eat all the fluffy ones. My dad always burns the last couple of batches." He shoved another malt ball in his mouth and took off down the steps.

Just then someone screamed so loud Roger and I nearly fell off the porch. We stared at each other. "Roger Huckleton, you are SO DEAD!"

"Sounds like Summer just discovered the rubber tarantula I hid in her fuzzy pink slippers. Sur-prise! Sur-prise!"

Like I said, driving Summer crazy is one of Roger's favorite activities. And he pretty much always gets in trouble for it. Seconds later, Mrs. H. started yelling for him.

I sighed and watched Roger vault over the hedge. It looked like our emergency meeting was officially over. I got up and banged through the back door into the house. It was up to me to figure out a way to get to—

"Lyons Island," my dad said. It was as if he had read my mind. I blinked and stopped in my tracks.

LION

The second-largest cat, after the tiger. The males have manes. The females hunt in packs. They live mostly in Africa.

". . . the garden party just started and the bathroom flooded," he said into his phone. "I don't know, but we'll have to go to Lyons Island right away. I'll pick you up in fifteen." He flipped his phone shut.

Whoa! My dad was going to Lyons Island!!!

"I forgot that party was today," said my mom. "I wonder if the expert will really be able to convince the mayor that—"

"Have you seen my new work gloves?" interrupted my dad. He pulled a yo-yo and a headless Barbie out of the drawer next to the fridge.

"In the microwave."

"Microwave?!"

"I was drying them. How are you going to get there?"

"We'll take Norman's boat. And by the way, these gloves are still wet."

"Oh," said my mom. "It was just an experiment. Next time I'll use the dryer."

I had to talk to Roger. We had no time to lose.

Less than an hour later, Roger and I were lying under a pile of blankets in the cabin of Uncle Norman's boat. It was hot and stuffy under there, and it smelled like perfume and fish. Even worse, every time the boat hit a wave, we rolled into each other.

We were stowaways . . .

"I'm suffocating," whispered Roger.

"Technically, you are not," I whispered back, "since you are getting some air through the blanket. To suffocate, you have to be completely deprived of oxygen and only inhale the carbon dioxide you exhale."

"Well, this sure is the stinkiest oxygen I ever inhaled." Roger pulled back the blanket and stuck his head out.

"Be careful."

Uncle Norman's boat wasn't big. In fact, the cabin was really just about big enough for Roger and me and a few fishing rods.

"Oh, man. They're eating lunch. I'm starving."

"Get back under here," I said. "They might see you."

"Just a sec." His arm shot out of the blankets and grabbed something, and then he wriggled back under. He took a bite and handed the rest to me. It was cold and wet.

"Mmm, mmm, good," said Roger. "Nothing like a dill pickle."

"Norm, did you eat my pickle?" my dad said a second later.

Roger and I looked at each other, eyes wide.

"No," said Uncle Norman. "Why?"

"It was here just a second ago."

Uncle Norman laughed. "You must have eaten it and forgotten."

"I sure don't remember eating it."

"Well, it had to be you because there's no one else here who could have, except a seagull, and we both know . . . "

"SEAGULLS DON'T EAT PICKLES!!!"

They laughed as if that was the funniest thing in the world. It happens to be true, by the way. See, seagulls will eat anything in the world except for pickles. Once when Uncle Norman was midnight fishing for stripers, he had a sandwich all wrapped up with a pickle. These seagulls landed on his boat and grabbed the whole thing. They gobbled up his turkey club—even the paper it was wrapped in. But they tossed the pickle right back.

Seconds later, I felt the blankets being yanked off. The sunlight was blinding. I had to blink a few times before I could see anything.

"Aha! It's the pickle thieves," said Uncle Norman. His lips were curling up like they wanted to smile. My dad had a big frown on his face.

"Hi, Dad," I said.

"And just what are you doing here?" My dad got right to the point.

"Well, you see, Mr. Finelli and Mr. Finelli..." Roger began.

"We just wanted to go for a . . . a . . . boat ride," I said before Roger could spill the beans about the treasure.

My father and Uncle Norman looked at each other and raised their eyebrows.

"Mr. Finelli, here's the rest of your pickle." Roger yanked it out of my hand and gave it to my dad.

My dad took a bite. "Since we don't have time to take you boys back, it looks like you're going to have to come with us."

I gave Roger the thumbs-up behind my back.

"Thanks, Dad," I said. "We didn't mean to be sneaky."

"Don't thank me," said my dad. "Uncle Norman and I should be thanking you."

Roger and I looked at each other.

"This is a big emergency, and we couldn't be happier to have two assistants to do the dirty work."

My dad winked at Uncle Norman.

"Dirty work?" repeated Roger.

He gave me the stink eye—you know, he bugged out his eyes and kind of closed one like he was going to wink. Then he scrunched up his nose and frowned, all at the same time.

"You'll see," said my dad. "Nothing like having some extra hands to help with the mess. Right, Fish?"

PLUMBERS, AHOY!

"Wait over there!" My dad pointed.

Roger and I carried mops, buckets, and toolboxes to the side porch.

"Whoa!" Roger looked around.

"Uh-huh!" I said.

The Lioness's backyard was huge. There were gardens everywhere with all kinds of flowers. There was a pond filled with koi, those fat orange fish that look like supersized goldfish, but they're really carp. An orchestra was playing. Waiters in uniforms walked around with trays of food and drinks. There were people dressed up in fancy clothes. In the very center was a giant ice sculpture.

"Boy, I sure wish I could take a chunk of ice off that eagle," said Roger. He wiped the sweat out of his eyes.

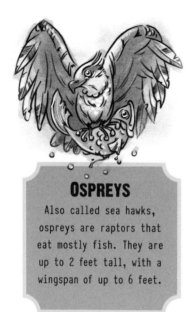

OSPREYS

Also called sea hawks, ospreys are raptors that eat mostly fish. They are up to 2 feet tall, with a wingspan of up to 6 feet.

"It's not an eagle," I said. "It's an osprey, also called a sea hawk. They're endangered, and Lyons Island has the largest population of—"

"You know who's endangered?" Roger interrupted. "Me! I'm about to faint from hunger and thirst."

A waiter passed by with a tray of tiny hot dogs. My stomach rumbled.

"Pigs in blankets are the best!" said Roger. "I could eat the whole tray."

My mouth watered.

"Excuse me!" Roger called out to the waiter.

"Roger!" I elbowed him.

"What? I'm hungry."

The waiter turned. Just then I saw the last person in the world I wanted to see.

"Yo-ho-ho, find the treasure yet?" asked Bryce. "I swear, that will be the easiest fifty bucks I ever make." He sauntered up to us with a nasty grin on his face. He was wearing his mirrored sunglasses and he was all dressed up in a white shirt and white pants. He snagged a pig in a blanket off the tray.

I glared at him.

"Gonna look for the treasure down the sewer?" Bryce pointed to the mops and plumbing supplies. "That's where you belong, with the rats and cockroaches."

I had to bite my lip so I wouldn't start yelling.

"Excuse me!" Roger called out to the waiter again.

"That food's not for you," said Bryce. "You weren't even invited to this party."

"How do you know?" I was starting to get mad.

"Duh!" said Bryce. "The plumbing equipment is a dead giveaway. I was invited because my dad's a successful real estate developer, and you weren't, because your dad's a dumb old plumber, so—"

"Take back what you said about my dad!" I glared at him.

"No way!" retorted Bryce. "Especially since it's true."

My ears started burning. I was so mad I felt as if my whole face was on fire.

"Is not!" I shouted. "Plumbers are supersmart. My dad knows all about engineering and math and—"

Heads turned. Conversations stopped. Waiters halted with trays in their hands.

Bryce just laughed. A waiter walked by carrying a tray of glasses filled with punch. Bryce reached for a glass.

"Whatever, loser! Just make sure you have my money ready, since you know I'm going to win the bet."

"You don't know that!" I yelled.

"Oh, yeah," smirked Bryce. He took a sip of punch. "Like you and your loser friends have a clue how to find that treasure."

"Quit calling us losers!" I said.

"Losers!" said Bryce.

Before I could think about what I was doing, I grabbed the closest weapon I could find. Then I stepped closer and waved the mop at him.

"Fish!" said Roger in a warning voice. "Don't."

"Oooh, a mop," sneered Bryce. "I'm so scared!"

He jabbed me in the chest with his finger. I was so mad that I pushed him back pretty hard. Bryce lost his balance and toppled backward right into the waiter. His glass of punch flew up in the air. The waiter's whole tray tipped. Punch got all over Bryce.

"I'm going to get you for this." Bryce's white outfit was splattered with red punch. It looked as if his clothes had developed a bad case of the chicken pox.

Someone gasped. Someone else laughed.

Before I could say a word, a stern voice said, "Boys, that's enough. This is a garden party, not a boxing ring."

I looked up into the icy blue eyes of an old lady dressed all in white. She wore a big white hat with big white flowers on it. *Oh, no!* It was the Lioness. My stomach felt like it dropped to my shoes.

"I'm sorry, ma'am."

She stared at me for a long moment. I wasn't sure if she even heard me. But before she walked away, I swear I saw her smile.

A little while later, my dad stuck his head out the door to tell us it was time to get started. Lucky for me, Bryce and the Lioness were nowhere in sight and the punch was cleaned up, so there was no evidence of the fight.

Roger and I followed my dad into the bathroom with the leak. We both stopped short.

I've seen a lot of plumbing problems in my life, but this one was such a mess it even made me forget all about big-mouth Bryce Billings. Not only had the toilet over-flowed, but the sink and bathtub had backed up, too. There was water and black goop all over the floor. The leak was so bad that part of the floor had sunk in.

"Let the games begin!" said Uncle Norman, handing Roger a mop.

My dad motioned me over to where he was busy unbolt-ing the toilet from the floor. I sighed and knelt down to open the black case and let out the snake. Don't worry—it wasn't a real snake. A snake is the coiled metal wire plumbers use to unclog pipes.

"Just a little farther," said my dad, after I had uncoiled almost the entire snake for him to send down the pipe. "Turn it again."

I sighed and turned the crank again. But whatever was stuck in the pipe was too far down for the snake to reach.

"Carmine, come on," said Uncle Norman. He stuck his head out from under the sink, where he was tightening a ring nut on a new section of pipe.

"Come on, what?" My dad pretended like he didn't know what Uncle Norman meant.

"This is the perfect time to try out the Zapper."

"Zapper?" asked Roger. He looked up from mopping the crud that leaked out when the toilet was unbolted. "Sounds dangerous."

"The Zapper 290 has a four-amp universal motor (*amp is short for ampere, which is the basic unit electric current is measured in, by the way*) and it's set to run at 325 RPM (*short for revolutions per minute*)," I explained. "It's for drains one and three-quarter inches to three inches wide, and the snake is one hundred feet long. It even takes pictures."

"Whoa, Fish, how do you know all that?" asked my dad as he pulled the snake back out of the pipe.

"Plumbing kind of runs in my family?" I joked. "Oh, and it cost a whopping—"

"Don't remind me," interrupted my dad.

"Remember the advertising?" asked Uncle Norman. "The Zapper goes where no snake has ever gone before."

The two of them cracked up. Plumbers have a weird sense of humor.

"All right, let's give the Zapper a try," said my dad. "Fish, run down to the basement and check the water valves."

I headed down the hall. The basement was just past

the kitchen. VROOM! VROOM! The Zapper sounded like a monster truck revving up for a rally. Its four-amp motor was really powerful.

I pulled back the bolt and opened the basement door. Just then I saw a flash of white behind me. I wondered if it was the Lioness. I turned. There was no one there.

I started down the steps. BANG! The door suddenly slammed shut. CLICK! The bolt slid into place. *Oh, no!*

I ran back up the steps. "Hey!" I shouted. "Open the door!" There was no answer. "Hey!"

"Gotcha!" taunted Bryce Billings from the other side.

"Let me out, Bryce!"

"I told you not to mess with me." Bryce laughed. "Later, gator."

I pounded on the door, but it was no use. Bryce was gone. And there was no way Roger, my dad, or Uncle Norman would ever hear me over the Zapper. I sighed and headed down the steps. I would just have to find another way out.

While I looked, I thought I'd better check the valves. I waded through boxes and old furniture. Chunks of ceiling and insulation had fallen from the leak. The water pipes were at the far end, sticking out beside a giant stuffed swordfish mounted on the wall.

I reached up and tightened the valves. Suddenly I heard a loud pinging sound, like someone was tapping a glass with a metal utensil. It was coming from the small window just above the fish.

PING! PING!

"A toast!" someone called out.

"Save Lyons Island!"

"Mr. E. Mann, director of the . . . *mumble mumble* . . . Captain Kidd . . . here at Lyons Island."

I stopped in my tracks. Mystery Man was the expert the Lioness had hired to save the island—but he was also hunting for the treasure? Something fishy was going on for sure. I climbed up on a trunk to hear better.

After the clapping, Mystery Man started talking. I couldn't catch every word, but it was stuff that I already knew—back in 1695, Captain Kidd had been hired by the English government to get rid of pirates, and King William III had even signed the order. Captain Kidd had overtaken a French galley that was filled with treasure from the South Seas. I couldn't hear what Mystery Man said next, except the words "trouble with the crew" and "diamonds." If only I could get closer to the window.

I jumped down and grabbed a box and stuck it on top of the trunk. Then I climbed up on the box. My head was now almost level with the window. I was also eyeball to eyeball with the dead swordfish.

"Captain Kidd was on his way home," Mystery Man said, "when he discovered there was a warrant out for his arrest. So he stopped at the closest place to hide the booty—Lyons Island. It is believed that the map of where he hid the treasure was itself hidden in a trunk that has his initials on it, plus a skull-and-crossbones symbol."

Whoa! That was exactly what T. J. said!

"The trunk is supposed to be of black wood and locked with an iron padlock," Mystery Man went on. "And in all these years, it has never been found. Legend has it that if anyone dared to open it, he would be haunted by Captain Kidd's ghost forever!"

BRRRRRMMMM! The hot-water heater started up with a bang. I jumped. I lost my balance. The box toppled over. I fell to the floor.

"Ouch!" I rubbed my head.

I leaned against the trunk. This one was black, just like the one Mystery Man was talking about. I noticed that it was locked with a rusty padlock that might be iron.

A shaft of yellow sunlight suddenly shone through the window, casting a stripe across the trunk. I blinked in surprise. There was none other than a skull and crossbones.

Oh, snap!

I jumped to my feet. There were two letters carved beside the skull and crossbones. One was a *W* and one was a *K.*

It was Captain Kidd's trunk!

Heart pounding, I tried pulling on the lock. It was stuck. I pulled harder. Still stuck. I reached in my pocket to see if I had a tool that might help. There beside the Superman Special Shooter marble I won off Two O and my library card was Grandpa Finelli's pocketknife. Carefully, I pushed the end of the spoon into the padlock. Then I shoved as hard as I could. No luck.

I shoved the spoon in again. CREAK! The lock popped open! I was so excited I could barely breathe. I opened the lid and peered inside.

The trunk was empty!

I kicked it in frustration.

POP!

Something shot out. It was a drawer.

Double snap!

It was a secret compartment! I had read about how sea captains and pirates hid valuable stuff in secret compartments and false bottoms in their trunks. I reached my hand inside. My fingertips touched something smooth and thin, like paper.

My heart started pounding. Slowly, I pulled out a rolled-up piece of parchment and stared at it.

Holy cow!

No one had touched this piece of paper since Captain Kidd hid it in this old trunk. So many people had hunted for it. Now, here it was in my hand.

Just then I heard something behind me. Mystery Man's words about Captain Kidd's ghost ran through my mind. Someone was watching me. Was it Captain Kidd? Was he upset I had the map? I stared around wildly, my heart beating a rat-tat-tat in my chest. But the only eye on me was the yellow glass eye of the dead swordfish. I took a deep breath. I had to calm down.

"Fish, are you down here?"

Footsteps thudded toward me. I stared at the parchment in my hand, just as my dad popped his head through the doorway. Now what?

I couldn't let my dad know I had found Captain Kidd's treasure map. I wasn't supposed to be looking for it in the first place. I couldn't put it back, either, because then Mystery Man might find it.

There was only one thing to do . . .

X MARKS THE–STOP!!!!

"You did *what?*" asked Roger. "No way!"

I nodded and paced back and forth across Roger's kitchen floor.

"But that's stealing," said T. J. He took a big bite of doughnut. Red jelly oozed out of the sides.

"Not exactly," I said. "Anyway, what else could I do?"

"Not take it," said Roger. "But since you did, let's check it out."

Carefully, I pulled the paper out from under my shirt. My hands were shaking.

T. J. took another bite of doughnut.

"How can you eat at a time like this?" I asked.

"Simple," said T. J. "I'm hungry." Powdered sugar shot out of his mouth.

"Watch the doughnut, dude!" I pushed my chair back from the table. "This is a historical document. It's worth tons of money. It's probably priceless."

"Dude, just unroll the map already," Roger cut in.

I took a deep breath. This was it. A pirate had held this very map in his hands. And it wasn't just any pirate. It was Captain Kidd, the pirate hunter. And now Roger, T. J., and I were going to find out where he had buried the most famous treasure in the whole world.

Just then Summer walked into the kitchen. "I'm hungry," she announced, pulling a brush through her long brown hair.

I shoved the map back under my shirt.

"Me, too. What do you want to eat?" T. J. jumped up and started opening cabinets.

I made a face at Roger. The treasure map felt like it was burning a hole in my chest. The suspense was killing me.

"Popcorn."

"Jiffy Pop is my favorite, too," agreed T. J. He watched hungrily as Summer took off the cardboard top and put the popcorn on the stove. The Huckletons don't have a microwave. Mrs. H. thinks the radiation is dangerous, even though I've told her all a microwave does is heat up the water and polarized molecules in the food.

Summer turned the flame on under the popcorn. At that moment, the phone rang. Roger picked it up. "Summer's French-Fried Eye-balls Cafe? Oh, hi, Beck—"

"Give that to me!" Summer yanked the phone out of Roger's hand and stormed out of the kitchen.

The coast was clear, so I pulled out the map. This was it. POP! POP! POP! went the popcorn as T. J. gave it a good shake.

MICROWAVE

In 1945, engineer Percy Spencer was working on a radar set when he noticed a candy bar in his pocket had melted. This gave him the idea for the microwave oven. It heats food by shoot-ing microwave beams that are absorbed by the water molecules in food. The first food to be heated successfully was popcorn. Microwave ovens for the home went on sale in 1967.

"Treasure map, take two," said Roger.

Carefully, I unrolled the crinkly old paper. I stared at it in surprise. I blinked once and then again. I couldn't believe my eyes.

"What, dude?" said Roger.

"Yeah," said T. J. "You don't look so good."

POP! POP! The tinfoil expanded and filled up with pop-corn. T. J. gave it another shake.

I didn't say a word. I couldn't.

"Let me see." Roger reached across the table and grabbed the parchment. "There's nothing written on this."

"I know," I said. "It's blank."

"How can it be blank?" T. J. moved toward the table. "Let me see that treasure map."

I thrust the piece of paper at him and jumped up. I needed a cold drink. I turned around and opened the fridge, looking for some orange juice. All I saw were bottles of this green seaweed stuff Mrs. H. likes.

"Quit calling it a treasure map! If there's no X to mark the—" I started.

"STOP!"

There was a scuffling sound and a bang. One of the chairs hit the floor.

I whipped around to see T. J. in front of the stove. He was holding the piece of parchment. His eyes were so wide I could see the whites all the way around. There was popcorn scattered across the counter and all over the floor. Roger stood beside him, his face pale.

"What happened?" I asked.

Neither of them said a word. They handed the piece of parchment to me. Only it wasn't blank anymore. There was a jagged outline of something that looked a whole lot like an island with trees marked out, and a rock—and there was a big X in the middle.

The treasure map!!!!

"Where did that map come from if the paper was blank?" asked T. J., breaking the silence.

Roger and I looked at each other. "Invisible ink!" we said at the same time.

"Huh?" said T. J. He shoved a handful of popcorn into his mouth.

"The popcorn!" Roger grinned. "Dropping the map on the Jiffy Pop was pure genius, T. J."

"If you write with certain liquids, like lemon juice, when the writing dries it becomes invisible," I explained. "Then it only becomes visible again if the paper it's written on is held over something hot, like a fire or a lightbulb."

"Or popcorn," Roger grinned and high-fived T. J. "Way to go, dude!"

"Invisible ink is one of the oldest methods of sending secret messages in the world," I said.

"Think Captain Kidd used lemon juice like we did?" Roger said. "He sure was one sneaky dude."

Just then a gust of wind blew into the kitchen and made the paper flutter. I shivered suddenly, remembering the story of Captain Kidd's ghost haunting whoever took the map.

A figure appeared in the doorway. It was dressed all in white, with a ghostly white face. *Oh, no!*

"Fish, are you all right, dude?" said Roger. "You look like you just saw a ghost."

Roger and T. J. turned around just as the ghost opened its mouth. "Is the popcorn done?" asked Summer.

"You know what, *Winter?*" teased Roger. "The abominable snowman look is really you."

It wasn't a ghost after all. It was just Summer in a white dress with white goop on her face. I had to stop being silly. Everyone knew there was no such thing as ghosts. . . .

CAPTAIN KIDD'S GHOST DOES NOT KID AROUND

"So, Nikola Tesla, what would you do if you were in my shoes?" I sprinkled some food into the fishbowl. "Not that you have feet to put shoes on. Would you dig up the treasure or return the map?"

Nikola Tesla's googly fish eyes goggled at me as he sucked up the food.

T. J. had voted to return the map to the Lioness. Roger thought we should dig up the treasure and then return it, because we would be heroes. I thought we should dig up the treasure, too. Then I would win the bet with Bryce. I couldn't wait to see the look on his face.

I quadruple-checked where I had hidden the map. It was right where it was the last three times I looked—on the top shelf of my bookcase in-side my diorama of the Stone Age. I had stuck the map in the Silly Putty cave where the woolly mammoth was being stabbed by two clay Stone Age people.

As I climbed into bed, Shrimp came into my room, jumped up, and plopped down on top of me.

"Ouch, Shrimp! Shove over!" I said.

He lay down across the bottom of my bed. I had to curl up my legs to make room for him.

"Night, Shrimp," I said, turning out the lamp on my dresser.

TAP! TAP! TAP! What was that sound? I rubbed the sleep out of my eyes. The moon was

NIKOLA TESLA (1856-1943)

An inventor born in what is now Croatia (that's in south-eastern Europe), Tesla invented early versions of the radio, the remote control, and radar. He also made "shadowgraphs," pictures of living tissue he took using electro-magnetic radiation (waves of energy associated with electric and magnetic fields), which were simi-lar to the first X-rays.

shining, making stripes of silvery light across the floor. There was a rustling noise outside the window.

Something was out there.

Something that was trying to get in!

It was Captain Kidd's ghost! It was coming to get me for taking the treasure map!!!

Shrimp growled and jumped to the floor. *Uh-oh!* I strained my ears, listening.

WHOOSH! A gust of wind blew into the room. There was a creaking, moaning sound.

GRRR! Shrimp growled again, his eyes trained on the window. The scream froze in my throat.

CREAK! MOAN!

My heart was beating so fast, it felt like it was going to jump right out of my chest. A shadow moved across the window. It looked like an arm. The long, bony arm of a skeleton.

TAP! TAP! TAP! The skeleton tapped on the window. It was the ghost. It was coming to get me. I pulled the pillow over my head.

A minute passed. And then another. Nothing happened. I peeked out. The room was lit up with moonlight again. The skeleton arm was still there, only it wasn't an arm at all. It was a tree branch!

Shrimp yawned and jumped back up on my bed. I yawned, too. Boy, was I crazy worrying about ghosts. I lay down beside him.

The next thing I knew, something sharp was poking me in the back.

"Give me the map, you scallywag!" yelled a gruff voice. "Or I'll run you through with my sword."

I gasped.

"Turn around and meet your doom," hissed the voice. "Or prepare to draw your last breath."

Slowly, I turned and found myself face-to-face with a ghostly pirate. His sword glinted sharply as he pointed it straight at my heart.

"Give me my treasure map, you cur!" he demanded in the same hissing voice. "For I am the ghost of Captain Kidd, and I do not kid around. . . ."

The ghost floated closer. His eyes blazed a terrible red and he let out a horrible moan. I could feel his stinky, rotten breath in my face.

Suddenly, something warm and wet dripped down my chin.

"Yuck!"

My eyes popped open. It was Shrimp! His head was on the pillow beside me. He licked me again. *Ugh!* Dog breath!!!

I sat up and looked around my room. It was morning. There was no ghost. I had dreamed the whole thing.

I hopped out of bed and hurried over to the diorama. The map was still there, sticking out of the Silly Putty cave.

Sure, I wanted to win the bet. Sure, I wanted to be a hero. But the right thing to do was to return the map to the Lioness. It wasn't because I was scared of Captain Kidd's ghost or anything. . . .

K-A-Y-A-K-S!

"Read my lips: N-O!" Roger turned on the hose to spray the dead-looking holly bushes in front of his house.

"Come on," I said. "Your dad never uses those K-A-Y-A-K-S."

It was the next morning, and I had come up with the perfect way for us to get to Lyons Island to return the treasure map. I just needed Roger to say yes.

"B-I-N-G-O!" said Roger. "My dad never uses them because they're O-L-D."

His dad also didn't use them because he doesn't live here anymore. He moved to California right after Roger's parents got divorced.

Roger started singing that annoying song about the Redwood Forest and the Gulf Stream waaa-aaaa-ters.

"Will you quit singing?!" I said.

"I can't," said Roger. "My mom thinks my beautiful voice will make the hollies so happy, they'll start to grow."

Mrs. Huckleton sure has some crazy ideas. "Doesn't your mom know it's the principles of photosynthesis that make plants grow, as in sunlight + water + carbon dioxide = photosynthesis = plants grow."

"Nah. She thinks it's that little four-letter word— L-O-V-E."

"Roger, come on," I said. "We have to get to Lyons Island pronto to return the treasure map. And K-A-Y-A-K-S are the way to go. I'll water the hollies and do your chores for a whole week."

Roger shook his head, but he stopped singing. I could tell he was listening.

"All right, I'll do your chores for two weeks."

"Okay, so long as you sing to the hollies, too," Roger said.

"Deal," I said. "Now, we better get going if we want to launch those kayaks before the tide rises."

We rode our bikes over to pick up T. J. and then stopped at the Captain's to get some PFDs. After that, we headed to the Point. We walked along the beach to the dock. The place was almost deserted, except for some kids poking in the sand for crabs. Mr. Huckleton's kayaks were tied at the end. Roger wasn't kidding when he said they were old.

"Are you sure this is a good idea?" asked T. J. He popped a piece of gum in his mouth. "These kayaks look kinda beat."

"I don't want to say I told you so," said Roger. "But I told you so."

"It's not like we're planning a cruise around the world," I said, although I had to admit they didn't look too good. "We're just going across the bay. And it's slack tide, so the water will be calm."

I stared at the line of scrub pines visible across the water. It was the closest Lyons Island came to Whooping Hollow. I knew from studying Uncle Norman's topographic maps (detailed maps that show the man-made and natural features of an area) that it was exactly 1.15 nautical miles away. I pulled my backpack up higher on my shoulder. Inside was the treasure map, triple-sealed in plastic baggies.

"Time to move out!"

"Double dibs on the one-man!" Roger called. He pointed to the smaller kayak, which also happened to be in way better condition.

"Okay," I said. They were Roger's dad's, so it was only fair.

T. J. and I pushed Roger off first. Then T. J. got in to steer while I pushed him off. WHOOSH! The kayak shot away.

"T. J., stop paddling!" I splashed over to the kayak and pulled myself in. The kayak tipped dangerously. "Paddle, T. J.!"

"But you just said to stop pad—"

"Just paddle!" I grabbed the other oar.

That's when I noticed the water in the bottom. That could only mean one thing. I spotted the leak right away. It was a wide crack in the wood on the starboard side, below the waterline. We would have to plug it up quickly if we didn't want to sink. But plug it up with what?

"How come you're not paddling?" asked T. J. He blew a big purple bubble with his gum.

"Gum—that's it!" I said. "T. J., you're a genius. Give me your gum!"

"Huh?" T. J. stared at me. He reached into his pocket and pulled out a twelve-pack of Banana Berry Blast bubblegum.

There were seven pieces left. I unwrapped one and popped it in my mouth, and then another and another and another.

"Hey! I didn't say you could have all of it!"

"Grumph me fyoors," I chewed, as I shoved the last three pieces in my mouth.

"I'm not giving you my gum," said T. J. "It's ABC gum. Remember what ABC means? Already Been Chewed!"

"I know!" I pulled the wad of gum from my mouth so I could talk. "Give me your gum. We have a leak, and if we don't want to sink, we have to plug it up with something. And gum, which happens to be made from rubber, is the perfect sealant."

"Oh," said T. J. He handed me his wad of purple gum. "You know, you're right about gum being like rubber, because sometimes when I chew gum, I feel like I'm chewing on my eraser."

I raised my eyebrows and kept chewing. Roger and I sometimes wondered if there was anything T. J. wouldn't eat.

"Hey, I want some gum!" shouted Roger, paddling toward us.

GUM

People have been chewing gum for thousands of years. It used to be made from tree sap. Now it's made from rubber (yep, rubber like an eraser).

"Can't," I said, spitting out my gum. "The kayak's got first dibs." I mashed my gum together with T. J.'s and shoved it into the crack.

"Whatever floats your boat!" Roger started to laugh.

And it did. Float our boat, that is, since the water stopped gushing in. Of course, I knew it wouldn't hold forever. Paddling was hard work, and my arms started aching. T. J. did his share of paddling, too, when he wasn't taking breaks to eat.

"Incoming!" Roger called to us.

T. J. and I both looked up. Coming our way was a whaler with a bright green stripe.

"Think it's Bryce?" I asked.

"Yep. Looks like they're heading our way. Get ready for contact. In ten . . . nine . . . eight . . ."

Roger didn't even make it to four before Bryce was close enough for us to hear him shouting, "Yo! Yo-ho-hos! Where do you losers think you're going in those sorry excuses for boats? Hope you have my money ready, Finelli, 'cause the two weeks is just about up."

"Get lost!" I yelled.

"I can't hear you!" Bryce turned the whaler so the bow was pointing in our direction. Then he pulled out the throttle. The engine revved and the boat zoomed right toward us.

"Oh, jeepo! He's going to run us over!" exclaimed T. J., his mouth full of chocolate-chip cookie.

"Mayday!" Roger waved his arms. "Mayday!"

He turned his kayak so the point, not the broadside, was facing the whaler. If you get hit broadside with a surge of wake when you're in a kayak, that means you're going for a swim.

"Paddle, T. J.!" We had to turn our kayak, too.

"Which way?" He gulped down another bite of cookie.

"Left! Quit eating and paddle!"

"Left?"

"Right! Hurry!"

T. J. paddled right. The boat spun in a circle.

"Not right, left!" I shouted.

"But you said right."

"I said left was right."

The whaler was getting closer and closer. Our kayak rocked from the waves. I could see Bryce's mirrored sunglasses glinting as he laughed at us. We had to turn the point into the wake right now, or we would tip for sure.

"Have a nice swim, losers!" said Bryce.

"Yeah, losers!" echoed Trippy.

"Turn your boat, guys!" said Roger.

But it was too late. A huge wave from the whaler's wake hit us hard broadside just as Bryce swerved the boat away.

"Aaahhhh!"

T. J. and I fell into the water. I came up spluttering but floating on account of the PFD.

Oh, no!! The backpack! I looked around frantically. It was bobbing just yards away. Luckily, the kayak had tipped 90 degrees and not 180 degrees, so it had already righted itself. T. J. was doggie-paddling beside it.

"Get the oars!" said Roger.

I lunged for mine just as the current was about to sweep it away. "Got it!"

"Got it!" T. J. said.

We climbed back into the boat. T. J. was eating a soggy-looking piece of cookie.

"Hey, T. J., where's your oar?"

"Dunno," said T. J. through a mouthful of cookie.

"But you said you got it."

"I meant my cookie. It was about to sink, but I got it just in time. Mint-chocolate-chip actually tastes kind of good with a little salt."

"Thar she blows!" pointed Roger.

T. J.'s oar was floating away in the general direction of the whaler, which was a small blur in the distance. At least we didn't have much farther to go. I pushed the gum more tightly into the crack.

We had gone less than a quarter of a mile when the gum stopped sticking altogether. Banana Berry Blast may be good gum, but it's no kind of long-term sealant.

"I was thinking," began T. J., shoving a fireball into his mouth, which was fiery red from the five fireballs he had already eaten. "We better be careful because we don't know for sure there isn't a lion on the island, so—"

"T. J., there is no lion, believe me," I cut in. "Now, quit talking and start bailing. The bottom's filling up again."

With a sigh, T. J. picked up his already sopping-wet baseball cap and started bailing out the water. It didn't do much good, but it was better than nothing.

"Land ho!" Roger called a little while later. "Let's beach these K-A-Y-A-K-S!"

THE MONSTER BIRD

T he three of us stood at the bottom of the front steps. The Lioness's big white house looked different than before. Maybe it was because the sun had gone behind a cloud and the place was in shadow. Or maybe it was just my guilt about the map. The black shutters almost felt like eyes watching us. And it was really quiet.

"Want us to go with you, dude?" asked Roger.

I shook my head. "Thanks, but it's a solo mission. I took the map, so I should be the one to return it."

T. J. handed me a bunch of fireballs. "These will give you courage." He popped a few more into his own mouth. He had eaten so many, I was surprised he didn't have smoke coming out of his ears.

I headed up the steps to the door and knocked with the big brass knocker. It was the shape of guess what? An osprey.

No answer.

I knocked again. Nothing. I peered through the glass pane beside the door. No one seemed to be around.

"Now what?" Roger asked.

"Wait and see, I guess."

So we sat on the steps and waited. The air was real heavy, the way it gets before it rains. We were sweating just sitting there.

"Fish, maybe we should come back another day," said Roger. He scratched a mosquito bite on his elbow.

"You could leave the map with a note," suggested T. J. "You know, like when your mom writes the teacher a note because your sister ate your homework or something."

"No kidding!" said Roger. "Mmm ate your homework?"

T. J. nodded. "It was a whole page of double-digit equations and everything. Mickey dared her."

"I'd like a plate of multiplication with mustard, hold the subtraction, please," joked Roger.

I whistled. I guess T. J. is not the only Mahoney who will eat anything.

"Leaving the map with a note isn't a bad idea," said Roger.

"I can't just leave the map," I said. "It's a valuable document. It could be blown away or lost or stolen."

"Stolen by who?" said Roger. "The flock of wild turkeys up in that tree? Gobble! Gobble! Gobble!"

T. J. laughed so hard, red fireball juice rolled down his chin.

Roger had a point. We couldn't wait all day. And there was the small problem of the leak in the kayak. We would have to plug it up if we wanted to get home at all.

"While we're waiting, we might as well fix the kayak," I said.

"With what?" said T. J. "I've got more fireballs because I bought the jumbo pack, but no more gum."

I frowned. We still had the old gum, but it was no good without something to actually fill the crack.

"What about we make a giant wad of spitballs?" joked Roger. "Or tie our shoelaces together, or—"

"That's it. Shoelaces!"

"Fish, I was kidding," said Roger. "Not even a great dodo brain like yours can come up with a way to fix a leaking boat with shoelaces. That's just crazy!"

"As a matter of fact, early shipbuilders used twine to

fill spaces and holes in the wood. Shoelaces might work, unless we find some real twine. Of course, if we want it to hold, we'll need a hammer to hammer it in. Then we can use the ABC gum to seal the twine, or shoelaces, in place."

"The Great Dodo Brain strikes again," said Roger.

"There's got to be a shed somewhere," I said. "You know, to keep all the gardening equipment and stuff."

EARLY SHIPBUILDING

On Viking ships, the planks were sealed with grass or animal hair. On early American ships, the planks were sometimes sealed with twine.

The three of us headed around the back of the house. We passed the gardens, the koi pond, a gazebo, and a swimming pool. There was a five-car garage, but it was locked. We walked what felt like a mile till we got to where the lawn ended. There was a pond, and beyond that, a bunch of pine trees. Right by the edge of the trees was a shed. We ran over and Roger knocked on the door. There was no answer. All we could hear were some crows cawing.

Roger turned the knob. "We're in, men!" He walked into the shed.

"Guys," said T. J., squirming. "I have to . . . um . . . you know . . ."

Roger and I looked at each other and raised our eyebrows.

"You know!" T. J. danced back and forth.

"Just go out to the woods, T. J.," I said, my eyes scanning the wall of tools for a hammer.

"Where?"

"Anywhere you want. It's not like there's anybody around."

There really wasn't anybody around. The caretaker must have been in town to get supplies. Now that I thought about it, that explained why the boat wasn't at the dock. And the rest of the staff seemed to be gone, too. They must have had the day off or something.

"Watch out for the lion," joked Roger.

T. J. turned back from the door.

"No worries, T. J.," I said. "He's just kidding. I told you Lyons Island is not a lion's natural habitat. Therefore you cannot be in danger from one unless it escaped from a circus, which is highly unlikely since it would have to swim all the way across the bay, and lions do not like to swim."

"But alligators do," said Roger. He jumped on top of a ride-on mower and gnashed his teeth and made roaring sounds.

"Don't listen to him," I told T. J. "Just go."

T. J. left, but he still looked uneasy.

"Check it out, Fish!" Roger bounced up and down on the seat of the mower. "It even has a cup holder. You could drink and mow at the same time. How cool is that?"

I didn't answer. I was busy looking for a hammer. I found one in an old toolbox under the workbench. Next, I went hunting for some rope.

"T. J.'s been gone a while," Roger said.

"I guess." I was busy looking through a drawer of empty plant containers. "Help me find some rope, will you?"

"Why didn't you tell me you needed rope? I was just making a lasso to rope that wild bull over there." Roger twirled a circle of rope over his head and aimed it at the wheelbarrow behind me. He missed.

"Will you quit fooling around—" I started to say, as Roger aimed the rope again. This time it landed around my shoulders.

"Olé!" Roger yelled. "Yippee! Yahoo!"

"Get that off me!" I yanked at the lasso. "Olé is for bull-fighting, dude, not roping bulls. Now, we just have to cut off a length of rope and—"

Suddenly we heard a scream. We ran outside. The screaming got louder.

"T. J.!"

The screaming seemed to be coming from the grove of pine trees just past the shed. We hurried through the trees. But he wasn't there. And the screaming had stopped.

We looked at each other, listening hard. Suddenly, it started up again, faint but unmistakable.

"That way!" I pointed to a forest of gum trees.

We dashed through the trees. Something swooped through the dim understory of the forest. But there was no sign of T. J.

"T. J.!"

Our voices echoed through the trees.

"T. J.!!!"

There was a muffled shout. It was coming from some-where ahead of us. Green moss hung like curtains from the branches. It took us a few minutes to push our way through. When we got to the other side, there was T. J. Gray and white goop dripped down his face.

"What happened to you?"

"This gigantic monster bird, like one of those dinosaur birds, came after me," said T. J. "I ran, and the next thing I knew it bombed me with this stuff."

"Where did this monster bird go?"

"That way!" T. J. pointed off into the trees.

Roger headed for the trees. I handed T. J. some leaves to clean himself up.

"T. J., that was no pterodactyl," I said, trying not to laugh. "It was an osprey and you got pooped, is all. There must be a nest around and it was just protecting its territory."

"All I see is flowers and a big blue rock," Roger called back to us. "No monster bird, dude."

Blue Rock? I thought. Why did that sound so familiar? I had heard that name before. *Blue Rock.* And then it hit me. I had not heard it. I had *read* it.

"No way!" My heart beat faster.

"No way what?" asked Roger. "You're surprised there is no monster bird?!"

I ran through the break in the trees. In the middle of a field of wild flowers was a blue-gray sandstone boulder.

"That's it!" I said, pointing at the boulder. "It's the first marker!"

"Huh?"

"Blue Rock is one of the markers on the map," I explained. "It's right near where the treasure is buried."

"Whoa!" said T. J.

"Not whoa!" said Roger. "Don't you mean, yo-ho-ho?!"

FIFTEEN FIREBALLS ON A DEAD MAN'S CHEST

I took out the map. The X was near a stream that ran almost the length of the island. I looked around the clearing. The stream was just across the field from us. *Bingo!*

So, the next question was, which direction was the X from the stream and Blue Rock? The map key didn't have NORTH at the top like usual. Instead, it was to the right, where EAST is supposed to be. Weird. Captain Kidd sure was tricky. If the key was correct, that meant the X was northwest of Blue Rock.

"So, are we ready to dig up the treasure?" asked Roger.

He and T. J. crowded around me to get a look at the map.

"Not yet." I frowned.

"Is it because you feel bad again about how you kind of stole the map?" said Roger.

"No!"

"Is it because you're afraid you can't? Don't be afraid! Look that fear in the eye, Fish. Tell it to make like a banana and split!"

Roger is always saying stuff like that. He gets these crazy ideas from the "find your inner power" CDs Mrs. H. likes to listen to. She says they help her sell houses.

"No! I'm not afraid of anything," I snapped. "It's just that there should be a third point." I jabbed my finger at the map. "See, the X where the treasure is buried is a certain distance and direction from the stream—or actually from the footbridge across the stream—the Blue Rock, and there should be one more marker."

"You mean like that tree," said Roger. He pointed to a small tree on the map that was east of Blue Rock.

I couldn't believe I had missed it. "Yes!" I looked at the map's legend. "According to this, it's a small white oak. So all we have to do is find it and then we'll know where the treasure is buried."

We looked around the clearing. There were lots of trees, but there was no small white oak.

"The only oak tree I see is that giant one over there." I sighed. "And that hasn't been a small tree for a long, long time."

"That's it!" yelled Roger. "When was this map made? Like, over three hundred years ago. So, a small oak tree would now be—"

"A big one!" We all high-fived.

"Okay, guys, we're ready to call the paces."

I pulled out my compass. "T. J., go stand at Blue Rock. Roger, you go over to the oak tree."

Roger raced to the tree, while T. J. munched his way over to the rock.

I checked the map and then ran over to the oak tree. "Okay, Roger, walk fifty-four paces southwest." I checked my compass and pointed him in the right direction. It seemed to take forever to count 54 steps, but finally he was standing in front of a clump of pricker bushes. I sure hoped the treasure wasn't buried under them.

"T. J., you have to go twenty-six paces northwest."

I raced over to T. J. with the compass. We walked the paces and wound up a few feet away from Roger and the pricker bushes. I dashed over to the crumbling stone bridge. I carefully walked twenty paces east toward T. J. and the rock. Then I walked thirty paces north.

The three of us stood looking at one another. There was an awful big space between us where the X was supposed to be.

"That's gonna be a whole lot of digging," said Roger.

I frowned. "The map is so detailed, the space should be way smaller."

"We did everything you said, Fish," said T. J., sucking on another fireball. "We walked all the paces, right?"

"Just like pirates," added Roger. "Ahoy, mateys, and heave-ho, and yo—"

"That's it!" I said. "Captain Kidd had longer legs than we do!"

So we walked the paces all over again, this time taking giant steps. When we were finished, the X where the treasure was buried was much smaller.

"X marks the spot!" I put down the backpack. "Now we just need some shovels and we can start digging!"

T. J. stayed to mark the spot. Roger and I hurried back to the shed. When we got there, we stopped to catch our breath. We stared up at the house. All quiet.

I thought I saw a light for a second at the top by the

widow's walk. I was about to point it out to Roger, but when I looked again, it was gone.

"Dude, what are you waiting for?" said Roger, pushing open the shed door.

We grabbed some shovels we found stacked up against one wall, along with an ice pick in case we hit rock, then raced back. T. J. was just where we had left him, still eating fireballs. I tossed him a shovel and the three of us got to work.

The ground was really hard. We had to keep using the pick to get rocks out of the way. It felt like hours had passed but we kept on digging. My arms started aching. I was hot, sweaty, and tired. I sure hoped the treasure wasn't buried much deeper.

"Sure you don't want a fireball?" T. J. asked for about the millionth time. He popped another one in his mouth.

"I don't know how you can eat those things," I said, wondering how deep we had gone. I figured about four feet.

"Yeah, dude, they can burn a hole right through your intestines and out your stomach," said Roger. "No joke."

T. J.'s eyes widened and he started to mumble. But his mouth was too full of fireballs for us to understand a word.

"Keep digging, guys," I said, tossing out another shovelful of dirt. The sky had gotten darker, and it looked like it might rain any second.

"Fish, I hate to rain on your parade," said Roger, grinning as he pointed up at the clouds. "But what if the treasure isn't really—"

Just then my shovel hit something hard. The three of us stared at one another. "Whoa! I think it's the treasure chest!"

Excitedly, we dug away the dirt. Sure enough, the edges of a chest began to appear. We pushed away the rest of the dirt with our hands. There in front of us was an old wooden trunk with a rusty padlock. Captain Kidd's treasure chest at last!!!

"Yo-ho-ho! Way to go!" whooped Roger.

"Woo-hoo!" I shouted.

"Yippee!" yelled T. J.

SPLAT! All the fireballs in his mouth landed right on top of Captain Kidd's trunk.

"Dude!" shouted Roger, jumping back from the fireball explosion.

"Oops!" said T. J. "I forgot you can't talk with fireballs in your mouth." He swallowed hard a few times and took a few deep breaths. He wiped up the mess with the bottom of his T-shirt.

"Man, T. J., I don't know how you can fit so many fireballs in your mouth," I said.

"Fifteen is my limit," said T. J.

"You know what they say?" joked Roger. "Fifteen fireballs on a dead man's chest. Yo-ho-ho and a—"

Suddenly there was a clap of thunder. It sounded like it was right over our heads. Lightning streaked across the sky.

"If we get zapped, we're toast," said Roger.

"Not necessarily," I said. "Lightning is more likely to strike the tallest things around, which in our case would be trees, not—"

"Forget the lightning, Fish. We are *so* toast," said T. J. "Look who's coming!"

Roger and I looked up. Our mouths dropped open. Striding toward us were Mystery Man and the librarian with the red glasses. And right behind them under a big white umbrella was none other than the Lioness.

"Not just toast. Burned toast with no butter or jam," said Roger. "That's us."

"White or wheat?" asked T. J.

"You look more like a burned bagel or cinnamon bun, if I had to pick a bread type," said Roger, who talks a lot when he's nervous. "Now, Fish would be a toaster pizza, and I would be . . . "

The surprise party of three reached us, and I took a deep breath. I was about to explain everything. Before I could even open my mouth, T. J. said, "See, I told you the partner was wearing a mood ring." He pointed to Red Glasses's hand. "When it turns red it means love, because she's in love with Mystery—"

"Mann!" Roger put in. "Mr. Mann, sir."

And everyone started talking at once.

HERE WE GO AGAIN!

A few days later, my dream came true. Roger, T. J., and I were lugging the Seagull motor down Main Street in Feenie's red wagon. We agreed to use the money we got as a reward for finding the treasure to buy the Seagull and fix up the Captain's boat. You probably want to know about the bet.

Hold on, I'm getting to that.

First, I need to tell you about the treasure. It sure wasn't what we expected. There were a bunch of old papers, a pair of long johns (I guess even pirates wear long underwear), and at the very bottom, a busted-up silver teapot and a bunch of silver spoons. That was it. No pieces of eight. No gold. No bars of silver. No diamonds or emeralds or rubies. Captain Kidd's real treasure is still hidden somewhere.

The good news is that Lyons Island is now a historic landmark, so the Lioness gets to keep it just the way it is. And T. J. was right about the mood ring and love and all that, because Mystery Man and Red Glasses—I mean, Ms. Valen—are engaged. They were very excited about the treasure. Old papers really are pirate booty to them. Mystery Man actually shook each of our hands and told us how impressed he was with our treasure hunting skills and our perseverance.

Turns out he is a real live treasure hunter. He actually went to where Captain Kidd's honest to goodness pirate ship, the *Quedagh Merchant*, was discovered off Catalina Island (that's in the Dominican Republic). And he went scuba diving to look for the treasure. There wasn't any. Just a bunch of old cannons. Captain Kidd's treasure is still out there somewhere. Mystery, I mean, Mr. Mann invited us to come to the library's Special Collection any time we want, and he framed a copy of the newspaper article about us finding the treasure and put it up in his office.

"Your turn," said Roger. He put the wagon handle in my hand just as we passed the library.

"Hey, did you ever pay that fine you owed?" asked T. J. He shoved an AirHead into his mouth.

"Mystery Man said I didn't have to," I said, grinning.

My library card was the clue that led Mystery Man and the Lioness to us. See, he found it in the Lioness's basement at the end of the garden party. It turned out that she remembered seeing a trunk like the one he talked about when the stuff in the basement got moved after the leak. So she and Mystery Man took a trip to the basement and found the same trunk I did. The next day (the day we dug up the treasure), he went to my house. Feenie told him I was on a hunt for "some kid's" treasure. Mystery Man put two and two together. Then he called the Lioness and met her in town and they hurried to the island to find us. The light I thought I saw at the top of the Lioness's house when Roger and I went to get the shovels really was a light. It was coming from the widow's walk, where Mystery Man and the Lioness were standing, looking for us, because you can see almost the whole island from up there.

Just then Roger nudged me. Rounding Town Pond were two boys. One of them was wearing mirrored sunglasses and pushing a red scooter.

"It's time, Finelli," said Roger.

All three of us started to run, pulling the wagon behind us. We caught up with Bryce and Trippy by the flagpole at the far end of the pond. It's a popular spot to watch the swans, or to bike and skateboard. There were a bunch of people there, but I barely noticed. I was too busy thinking about what I was going to say to Bryce.

"Hey, Bryce!" I called.

"Yeah, loser," Bryce sneered.

"I won the bet!"

"Yeah, Bryce," Roger piped up. "Fish found the treasure, so he wins."

"It's been more than two weeks," said Trippy.

"I know," I said. "But the day we found the treasure was the fourteenth day. So it was exactly two weeks."

By this time, a bunch of people were watching. There were some kids from our class and a group of older kids from Marine Middle, including Roger's sister, Summer, and Beck Billings. At the very back of the crowd was my mom. She was holding a loaf of bread that Feenie and Mmm were feeding to the cygnets. Everyone had their eyes on us.

"It's all over, Bryce," said Roger. "Fish found the treasure. Now give him the sunglasses."

Bryce frowned and looked at Trippy, who shrugged.

"He found Captain Kidd's treasure in two weeks, just like he said," Roger went on. "That means he wins. So give Fish the sunglasses."

"Give Fish the sunglasses!" someone in the crowd yelled.

"Give Fish the sunglasses!" called another voice.

Bryce had no choice. A bet was a bet, and I had won it fair and square.

Reluctantly Bryce pulled off his mirrored sunglasses. He threw them at me and I caught them.

"Put them on." Roger nudged me.

So I did, and everyone clapped. Feenie and Mmm waved their magic wands. My mom smiled. So did Summer. The crowd started breaking up.

"It's just a pair of sunglasses," said Bryce. "It's no big deal. You're still a loser." He nodded toward the wagon. "You gonna fix your dad's broken-down truck with that old motor?"

"For your information, this engine isn't for a car or a truck at all. It's a Seagull motor, one of the finest motorboat engines ever made. The British used them to power light assault craft during World War II, as a matter of fact."

"Read my lips! Who cares?" said Bryce.

"You will, when we use it to bury you at the Captain Kidd Classic."

Bryce snorted. "Beat me? With that old thing? You must be kidding."

"No, I'm not kidding. We're not just going to beat you. We're going to win the Silver Cup."

"Oh, yeah?"

"Yeah!"

"I dare you, Fish Finelli," said Bryce. "I double-doggie dare you."

"Just you wait! You'll be eating our spray."

Roger and T. J. looked at me, eyes wide. I knew they were thinking of Bryce's brand-new whaler. His top-of-the-line, superlight, super fast boat with the 9.9-horsepower Mercury FourStroke engine.

"You losers must be kidding," said Bryce. "You couldn't beat a canoe with your old boat."

"Just watch us!" I said.

"*The Fireball* can beat anything," said Roger.

"Later, losers!" said Bryce, as he and Trippy walked away.

"*Fireball?*" T. J. and I both looked at Roger.

"Great name for our boat, right! Remember what happened when we dug up Captain Kidd's trunk?!"

I smiled. *"The Fireball.* I like it."

"Oh, you mean when I . . . " T. J.'s voice trailed off. "I get it!"

Roger whooped and held up his hand. T. J. and I started whooping, too.

We did our secret handshake. And we said our secret password—"S.D.E.P."—and bumped fists.

"Here we go again," said Roger.